# Sun in My Heart

*A Contemporary Romance with a Twist*

Tricia T. LaRochelle

FLAMING HEART PRESS

This book is a work of fiction. Names, characters, and incidents are either products of the author's imagination or are used fictitiously.

Manufactured in the United States of America

Copyright © 2023 by Tricia T. LaRochelle

ISBN 979-8-9861756-8-3 (paperback)

ISBN 979-8-9861756-7-6 (ebook)



Published by Flaming Heart Press, United States of America

Distributed by Ingram Book Group

Cover design by Damonza

 Created with Vellum

# Praise for Tricia T. LaRochelle

*Sun in My Heart*, Bronze Medal winner in the 2024 Readers' Favorite contest for Romance - New Adult.

*Sun in My Heart*, Second-place winner in the 2024 Bookfest Awards for Romance, Contemporary Romance, New Adult.

*Flickering Heart* (Book 1 in the Sara Browne Series), Gold Medal winner in the 2023 Readers' Favorite Contest for Fiction - New Adult.

*Flickering Heart*, first-place winner in the 2022 Incipere Awards for Romance.

*Revive* (Book 2 in the Sara Browne Series) Honorable Mention winner in the 2022 Incipere Awards for Romance.

"Tricia T. LaRochelle's *Sun in My Heart* is an emotional rollercoaster, a story skillfully crafted to keep readers engaged and invested in the lives of the characters. The narrative weaves complex relationships, familial dynamics, and personal secrets into a thrilling tale of survival, resilience, and the healing power of love."
—Readers' Favorite

"LaRochelle skillfully envelops readers in a poignant, romantic story tinged with tension and intrigue in her latest novel *Sun in My Heart*. A stirring celebration of the bonds of love, family, and friendship, this is a surefire winner."
—Prairies Book Review

"LaRochelle writes like a pro and delivers a profoundly entertaining romance story with genuinely flawed characters and a deftly handled plot with explosive moments."
—The Book Commentary

*I dedicate this book to anyone who falls victim to violence of any kind. May you escape your bonds and find a better path.*

# Sun in My Heart

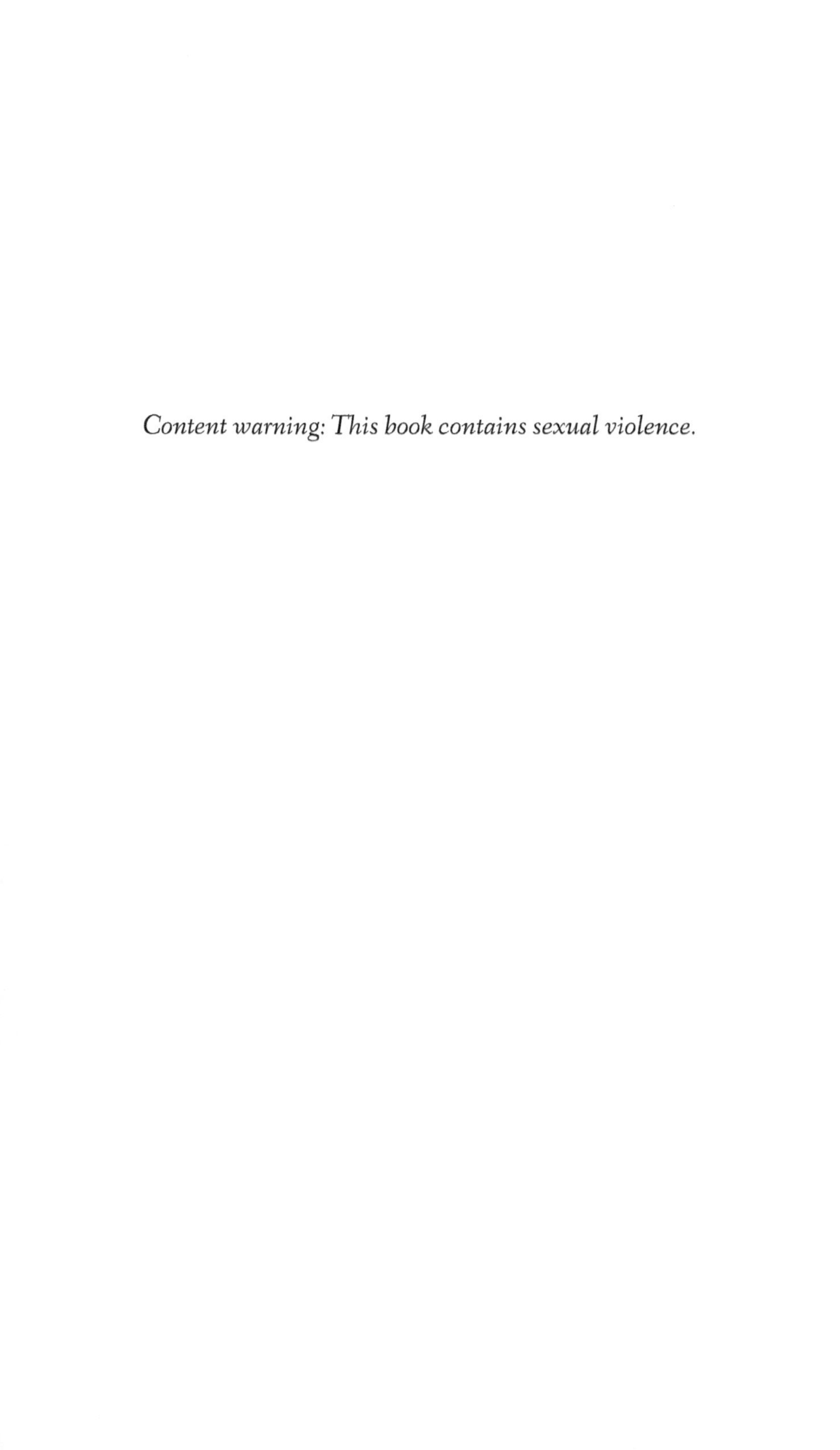

*Content warning: This book contains sexual violence.*

# Chapter One

Julian awoke feeling as if a cannon were going off inside of his head. A cannon? More like a marching band equipped with nothing but snare drums. He struggled to swallow, his mouth as dry as a California desert.

"Jesus," he said as he sat up in bed, rubbing his bloodshot eyes and trying to gain focus, his dark, shoulder-length hair brushing over his bare shoulders.

"What the fuck did I drink last night?" Julian asked to no one in particular, a burp coated with old whiskey forging its way up his throat. Next to his bed, a glass containing the remnants of the amber liquid sat on his nightstand, mocking him. And then he remembered the pills and the blow, the edges of his brain replaying several short, blurry images of last night's party.

A woman stirred next to him, her long, red hair draped over her pillow resembling a shih tzu in need of a grooming. One of her large breasts peeked out from under the sheet. She half moaned as she rolled onto her stomach, breathing deep and rhythmic.

Julian racked his brain. *Sheila? Susanna?*

Feeling like he'd just encountered the hood of a truck, one that was pushing eighty miles an hour, Julian gazed around the room, the air primed with old cigarettes, weed, booze, and a contradictory whiff of flowery perfume wafting off the woman lying next to him.

He exhaled, rubbing his forehead, the morning light bringing clarity into the opulent 2,200-square-foot hotel suite equipped with marble floors and a private swimming pool. Empty bottles, cups, room service trays, and used clothing (mostly his) cluttered the tables, chairs, and floor.

Outside a wall of windows, the Las Vegas strip awaited, its lights diminished by the late afternoon sun's rays. Soon, the sun would relent, bringing rebirth to the nighttime sky. And that was when Julian would shine for his nearly 30,000 fans, a smaller crowd compared to most he performed for.

How had he gotten here? Just a few short years ago, Julian was playing for small crowds, his trusty acoustic guitar resting on his lap, providing just the right amount of melody for his folk songs. His jeans were worn, his T-shirts equally weathered. He wasn't a rock star or a celebrity, and he was okay with that, playing what he loved and connecting with his audience. All five of them, if he was being honest. He wrote his own songs and made his own arrangements, which usually consisted of a bug-infested hotel room or the back of a van provided by one of his bandmates.

That all changed when a talent scout showed up one night, liked what he heard, and the rest, as they say, was history—if history included screaming crowds, five-star accommodations, limos, bossy managers, and all the drugs and alcohol he could ingest. And then there were the women, each one eager to give him exactly what he wanted—no holds barred—and as often as he liked. What did they want in return? A moment with a pop star. A taste of celebrity. And bragging rights for the rest of their lives.

Last month, he turned thirty-one, but at that moment, Julian felt more like ninety. An uncomfortable sweat crept over his chest, forcing him to throw the sheets off and dangle his legs over the side of the mattress, his nakedness on full display. At least the room wasn't flooded with a barrage of passed-out partiers, fans, and a few band members. It was mostly empty, save for the woman lying next to him, who he could barely remember, and the one he had just noticed sitting on the sofa across from the foot of his bed, smoking a cigarette and boring a hole through him with her dark-brown eyes.

"What are *you* doing here? How'd you get in?" Julian said, looking around the room in disgust.

Fire brewed in her eyes. The young woman sat motionless, her bleached blonde hair stringy and in need of a shampoo. Her makeup smeared across her cheeks from crying, no doubt.

*Not this again.*

Julian knew this woman all too well, and she certainly knew him. Her name was Rebecca. She'd been stalking him for the past six months, trying for a hookup. And the girl was persistent, which told Julian right away to steer clear. And he *had* whenever he'd encountered her outside of a backstage door, in the lobby of his hotel, or even in his bed once after he'd returned from a concert. She'd stolen clothes and trinkets, and when Julian hired security to guard himself against her, she'd hacked into his social media accounts, forcing him to shut them all down. The girl couldn't have been a day over eighteen, and no matter how much she begged and offered to do anything he wanted sexually or otherwise, he wasn't tapping that. Rocking the cradle had never been his style. Neither had screwing crazy women.

"Listen, Rebecc—"

"No! I'm done listenin'," she said, tears running down her cheeks, creating a tributary toward her mouth, mucus from her nose thickening her river of heartache. Dark makeup smudged under her eyes, horrifying her appearance. "You won't fuck me, but you'll fuck her?" With one of her hands extended, her eyes filled with distress, Rebecca zeroed in on the redhead. "I'm better than her. I'm better than all of them. Why can't you see that?" Her voice settled into a terrifying purr. "I'm good for you, baby. You need me. None of them can take care of you like I can. That last song you wrote, I knew it was for me."

The song she was referring to was titled "Sunshine," and although it was about women and the joy they brought into Julian's life, it wasn't about any one person in particular. All their names blurred together. Yes, Julian slept around, and this was his way of thanking all the ladies who had inhabited his bed, shower, floor, tour bus, and everywhere else he'd *enjoyed* their company. Who the song *wasn't* about was Rebecca, who was Kathy Bates to his James Caan in the movie *Misery*. Just like Annie Wilkes, Rebecca saw what she wanted to see—or more accurately—heard what she wanted to hear.

Julian shook his head, his hand flying to his forehead to stop the throbbing from within his brain. Why didn't he press charges the last time she'd pulled this? She was young, and something told him she was alone. He even tried to get help for her, and that's when she disappeared.

Still, he should have been more careful, maybe not telling his security team he didn't need them after Rebecca had stopped her antics two months ago.

He draped a portion of the sheet over his lap and took a breath, not in the mood for this psychobabble or whatever was about to happen. After two quiet months without Rebecca's shenanigans, he thought she'd moved on. Or so he'd hoped.

"Rebecca. You need help. I told you if you didn't stay away from me, I was going to call—"

"Who? The cops? You think I care about that?"

The redhead lying next to Julian turned over and sat up, covering her upper half with the same sheet covering Julian's lower. "What's going on?" she asked, her eyes trying to make sense of the scene before her. "Is this your wife or something?" Her voice carried a bucketload of outrage.

Julian shook his head vehemently as Rebecca burst into a fit of crazed laughter.

"You think I'm his wife? See, even *she* sees what we mean to each other. Why can't you? I need you, Julian. I know you love me. You think I'm too young, but you're wrong. I'm perfect for you."

Bile rose in the back of Julian's mouth as he raised a palm to stop her from ranting. He'd heard it all. "Rebecca, please listen to me. You have to stop this reckless behavior. Nothing is going to happen between us. But I have connections. You need help, and I can make that happen for you."

Before he could say any more, Rebecca shook her head from side to side like a toddler refusing to eat her vegetables. "Don't." Her lips tightened into a thin line, her cheeks raging with pink fury. "Don't tell me what I need." And then she pulled a gun out of her coat pocket.

*Fuck, no.* This was so much worse than Julian had imagined.

Eyes expanding to the size of saucers, the woman sitting next to him screamed and pulled back against the headboard, her body stiff, the sheet doing its best to shield her.

Julian patted her arm. "It's okay. She's not going to—"

"No one is going to take you away from me. No. One!" The gun exploded, not giving Julian enough time to react or protect himself. Clumps of brain matter and blood coated the side of his face, shoulder, and the bed sheets below. The ghastly image made Julian vomit on the spot, the contents of his stomach puddling on the floor next to his bed. He convulsed, his muscles tight and terrified.

When Julian finally dared to look back at Rebecca, he couldn't discern what she was feeling or thinking at that moment, her eyes blank, her expression unusually calm. "Are you nuts?" Julian grabbed the redhead and slid her down onto her back, her large breasts flopping around like water balloons. Wiping her mouth clean as best he could, he performed CPR, but her lungs refused the oxygen, her eyes open and devoid of life. For the love of God, half of her brain was missing. The metallic taste left behind in his mouth provoked his stomach to hurl once again.

He'd never seen death up close, not like this. And he'd never been on the other side of a gun, either. Was Rebecca going to kill him next? His entire body shuddered, his stomach leaping into his throat, the acids burning everything in its path. His beating heart and rapid pulse had exorcised the hangover from his body.

Julian began to weep, panting and praying that someone, anyone, had heard the gunshot and would burst through the door to help. "What have you done, Rebecca? She did nothing to you. You didn't even know her."

Rebecca's face turned to stone, her voice as cold as an iceberg. "Neither did you. You're never going to let me in, are you? You're never going to give me a chance." Her tone remained eerily calm.

*Let you in?* Even though he'd told her a thousand times that wasn't going to happen, he held his tongue, the one that tasted like barf and blood, and begged for water.

In direct contrast to Julian's near hyperventilating lungs,

Rebecca behaved almost peacefully, as if none of the carnage before her had any effect. The chick had lost it.

Julian ran a hand down his face, his insides quaking with fear. He could barely breathe. "Please, Rebecca," he wheezed. "I didn't mean to hurt you. We can talk. For as long as you want." He raised his palms as a gesture of surrender. "Just please put the gun down."

A sardonic grin swept across the young woman's face. "You and I both know that that is *not* going to happen. It's over. They will never let me anywhere near you now. We only have a few minutes left." She switched the pistol from one hand to another and then back again like someone would do with a small ball.

*What is she doing? Toying with me?* Julian remembered all the times his father had brought him to the shooting range. Growing up with a marine for a father, he'd learned a great deal about his dad's training. It took Julian years to convince his father that he was a singer, not a fighter, but the training persisted anyway. "*With people shootin' each other left and right these days, you need to know how to handle a gun, son,*" his dad had said over and over again until it stuck.

Those memories rose up Julian's spine, flooding it with courage where there wasn't any. And then, he problem-solved the situation as best he could.

Rebecca sat across the room, which meant there was no time to lunge for the gun, not without risking her firing it first. And judging by the crater she'd just gouged through the redhead's forehead, Rebecca was a good shot. Julian owned a gun, too, but he didn't have it with him. That was dumb. He knew better. His father had tried to tell him.

"Why? Julian? Why don't you love me?" Tears swarmed Rebecca's cheeks once again. She tapped the gun against the side of her head, the sound making a revolting clank against her skull.

Julian knew he was next if he didn't think of something to de-escalate the situation. He'd be dead within minutes. *Keep her talking.*

"I do love you, Rebecca. You're young. And I can't be with someone who is so much younger than I am. It wouldn't be right. That's all this is. It's not you. You're a beautiful girl. I'm sure lots of guys—"

"Don't you dare patronize me. And I am not a girl. I am a *woman.*" Her eyes brewed with newfound ire. "You *don't* love me." And then, just like that, her face melted into a sobbing mess, her lip quivering. "No one does."

*What happened to you? Who made you this way?*

"That's not true. I do care about you. I promise I do. And I can get you help. Please. Just let me."

"This is the only way I can possess your mind. You won't let me in any other way. I have no other choice. I will haunt you for the rest of your pathetic life. And you will *never* forget me. Goodbye, Julian."

A second bullet exploded from the gun's chamber.

# Chapter Two

"Recent reports that pop singer Julian Sommers was spotted recently at a Starbucks in the heart of LA turned out to be false. Sources tell *Entertainment News* that the man they thought was Julian was not, in fact, him." The dark-skinned reporter with a flawless complexion and perfect hair smiled as she spoke, her teeth so white they glowed. "After a sizzling start to his career as a pop star, Julian Sommers faced off with a young woman who he claimed had been stalking him for months. It was during an altercation in his Vegas hotel room two years ago, the young woman became violent, shooting Julian's companion before turning the gun on herself. A lengthy investigation followed, and police cleared Julian of any wrongdoing. Since then, *Entertainment News* has been trying to locate the fallen pop star for an interview. With no clues to his whereabouts, the question remains: 'Where in the world is Julian Sommers?' which is the name of our new segment. Stay tuned for updates. This is Lisa Pantera, reporting live for *Entertainment News*."

Sophie stared at the gorgeous pop singer with glacial blue

eyes in awe. She could understand how a fan could go a little nuts over a hottie like him. Blessed with a strong jawline and expressive eyes, he had a smile she was sure dazzled his fans. His brown, shoulder-length hair shined in the photo on the TV, his bangs brushed over to one side just enough to look casual, a few wisps of caramel strands adding dimension. The stock photo *Entertainment News* chose to use didn't reveal much of his body, but his shoulders and neck looked strong and yummy. Not that Sophie was pining over the guy. She'd had enough of men for a while. A long while.

Her ringtone interrupted the broadcast. She clicked the show off and reached for her phone, grumbling to herself when she saw who was calling. Within seconds, Sophie's defenses were up.

"Yes, Mom, I hear you. How many times are you going to tell me that?"

From the other end of the line, a huff forced its way through, one laced with repugnance. "Since you keep forgetting to show up, I'd say I'm not reminding you nearly enough. Your ungrateful attitude is both childish and insulting. Your father was expecting you at that party."

Sophie and her mother were not on what you'd call the best of terms. Since birth (if you asked Sophie), her mother, Cecilia, had always found something to criticize about her one-and-only daughter. If Sophie gained a few pounds, her mother made cracks about it. If Sophie's grades slipped, her mother ridiculed her. It seemed to Sophie that she couldn't do anything right: *"What in the world are you wearing?" "Why are you hanging out with those people?" "Stop embarrassing this family."* Her mother's so-called observations filled Sophie's ears with verbal muck on a regular basis. And it had been that way for the past twenty-three years.

Her parents' parties were all about status and intention.

This most recent event, which was more of a fundraiser than anything else, was a good example. Sophie's father was what you'd call a bigwig in the corporate world. Johnathan Quinn owned a sizable construction company, a heavy machinery rental business, and a budding investment firm that was growing like a weed by the day. What did her mother do? Spend. Even more than Sophie's father, Cecilia also liked to entertain, and entertain she did, any chance she got. It provided her with the perfect excuse to show off her new outfits, luxury estate, and the impressive grounds surrounding it. And they *were* impressive, enough to warrant a full-time gardener and pool staff.

"I said, 'Your father was expecting you.' Are you even listening to me?" Cecilia kept her tone clipped and to the point. Sophie could almost hear the invisible scissors in her ear.

This was how most of their conversations went. The disappointment in her mother's tone needled Sophie so much she could almost see the pinpricks on her skin. Why did they care if she was there or not? She didn't even know these people.

"*Dad* was expecting me? Did he even show up? Last time I was there, he never came." That was another sticky subject within the Quinn family household: when and where her father chose to make an appearance. The comment was a barb, and Sophie knew it, and so unlike her. But when it came to her mother, her claws had a mind of their own.

A moment of stressful silence sparked like friction between mother and daughter. "Well, that couldn't be helped. He had some last-minute ... obligations." The way Sophie's mother spoke, Sophie imagined her gritting her teeth while she said those words like she always did when her father did something that upset her.

Meetings and business trips governed Johnathan's schedule, but Sophie suspected that wasn't always the case, like when he'd slipped up and told them he was in one location, but they'd found out otherwise. It happened six months before she married Chad, and it happened when Sophie had crashed her BMW into a telephone pole. Rain fell from the sky in buckets that day, and her vehicle had hydroplaned. Even though the police deemed it an accident, brought on by foul weather—and even though Sophie wasn't speeding at the time—Cecilia used it as yet another opportunity to scold Sophie for being ... well, Sophie—which meant *far* from perfect.

Unable to reach her father by cell, Sophie called the hotel on speaker phone, hoping to talk with her dad about what had transpired. But the reservation clerk said he wasn't staying there, even though that was precisely where, according to her mother, he'd said he'd be. "*I'll be at the banking expo all weekend long,*" were his exact words. "*I've got some high-powered meetings lined up, so please try not to disturb.*" Her mother had recited the message with pinpoint clarity.

According to that same hotel clerk, the only conference in town that weekend was something called The Apex Beauty Experience, held for salon owners, beauty consultants, and vendors. The polar opposite of construction and investment. And since his cell went right to voice mail *every* time they tried it, they weren't able to tell him about the accident until he returned home several days later. They could have left a message, but her mother refused, her face stretched tight like a balloon ready to pop.

A little banged up at the time, and since Chad was also out of town, Sophie chose to stay in her old bedroom, where she couldn't escape her mother's perma-frown that rode like a storm all the way up to her angry blue eyes. Her recent facelift fought hard against any new wrinkle lines, determined to bring some form of expression to her expensive face. Her skin was like plastic, but her eyes smoldered like no other. And even though Sophie pitied her mother during those moments, she also feared her. Cecilia wasn't a violent woman, but if you got on her bad side, you paid the price.

That night, they ate dinner in the formal dining room and breakfast in the expansive kitchen the next morning, neither one of them saying a word, only a few sighs escaping from her mother's pursed lips, the clock ticking like a gong against the deafening silence. Even the cook staff and housekeepers steered clear.

All weekend, tension and frustration fumigated every inch of their house, and Sophie knew why: This wasn't the first time her father had been duplicitous about his whereabouts. On the one hand, she could understand her dad's need for human companionship, something her mother refused to offer. But on the other, it was wrong of him to cheat, especially when he could have just divorced her, for crying out loud.

Apathy governed Cecilia's voice, and Sophie imagined her bored, staring at her nails or straightening a few wisps of blonde hair around her eyes. "Your father is hosting some new investors next week, and he'd like his family here to support him. I expect you to be here *and* wearing something presentable. None of those rags I always see you in." She made a *tsking* with her tongue. "Honestly, it's almost as if you wished you were poor."

"I'm not wearing a gown, Mother! And who are *these* people?"

"I said they are investors."

"Investors for what?"

From both locations, anger pinged back and forth off the cell towers like a cutthroat tennis match.

"What difference does it make? You will be here, or else."

That was another thing Cecilia liked to do: threaten. *"I'll take your car away." "I'll freeze your bank accounts." "I'll have you kicked out of that expensive townhouse your father pays for.*"

The truth was, Sophie didn't care about any of those things, which was why she sold her expensive SUV and bought a sensible car, got a good job at a nonprofit that helped low-income mothers find employment and proper housing, and moved to a modest-sized cottage in the country, sixty miles west from her parents' estate in Richmond, Virginia. She used her own money this time, not Daddy's.

All of this happened *after* she left Chad.

"Is Chad going to be there?" Sophie hated to ask, but at the same time, she needed to know.

Her mother's tone lifted. "Of course. He's your father's new VP. Why wouldn't he be here? He's family."

The acids in Sophie's stomach roiled, irritating her throat.

The only time Cecilia approved of anything that Sophie had done in her life was when she had married Chad, a popular boy in high school *and* college and a VP in her father's expanding investment firm. Chad was good at math and terrible at human compassion. If Cecilia had borne a son, Sophie suspected he would have come out just like Chad. He was cold, determined, and abusive, to say the least. Although he didn't seem that way at first.

But Cecilia didn't have a son. She had a daughter, one who she couldn't relate to.

"I'm not going if he's there. And he's *not* family. We're separated, Mother, remember? It's been six months." Sophie's chest tightened, her lower lip starting to quiver.

"Yes, you are. Your father doesn't know about your problems, and he's not going to find out. Not until you get your act together and start behaving like a responsible human being."

She was right. Sophie's father didn't know why she had left town. She wasn't even sure he knew she was gone, or where she slept these days. And Sophie was in no hurry to tell him about it. For now, fighting with her mother was enough. She didn't need both of them coming down on her about her failed marriage. These days, she barely spoke to her dad anyway. The man was disconnected—from everything except for his business dealings. When it came to that, he was a shark. On top of everything, twenty-four seven.

Cecilia exhaled loudly. "When are you going to come to your senses? Chad is the best thing for you *and* for this family. And I refuse to cast him out because you can't get along with your husband—or anyone for that matter. You're not a child anymore, Sophie. It's time you started acting like it."

Tears stung Sophie's eyes, but she willed them back into hiding. "He was abusive, Moth—"

"I don't have time for these childish games. I'm meeting the mayor's wife for lunch in forty-five minutes."

*Click*, the phone severed the call.

Sophie plopped down on her comfy persimmon-colored sofa and rested her head back, trying to center her emotions. She grabbed one of her floral accent pillows to hug for support, her feet finding respite on the matching oversized ottoman. She inhaled the room, the tuberose offering scents of crème brûlée and honey to the air.

She loved her little cottage that she'd decorated with plantation blinds, coffered ceilings, and seven-inch oak floors. Her kitchen was small, but the island made of white marble, along with the perimeter countertops provided plenty of room to construct her meals for one. She'd splurged on the mosaic backsplash behind the cooktop and made sure she had top-of-the-line appliances, including a small wine fridge that blended with the white cabinets like family. When she'd bought the place, it was a wreck, but watching her mother decorate and remodel her family home for years, she knew who to contact to get the job done.

If only she could fix her personal life that easily—go back in time and counsel her younger self, she wouldn't find herself in this predicament.

Despite her absent father and her overly critical mother, and despite her privileged childhood, Sophie considered herself a good person. But not smart when it came to men. It was in college, during one of her psychology classes, that she finally put two and two together and realized why. Trying to fill the void from nonexistent and unloving parents, Sophie sought affection elsewhere. And since she came from money, Sophie was thrust in with the popular kids, who were a whole different breed of animal. Yes, she slept around in high school, but no more than any of the other trust fund bitches. The problem was she couldn't relate to any of those girls. They had a tendency to stop talking whenever she approached. The fact that every now and then, she'd also hear the nickname *Gollum* float past her ears didn't help matters, a few giggles accompanying it. Sophie's eyes were hazel, and they were large; she knew that. But she wasn't Gollum, and they were assholes to call her that.

Over time, she befriended the ones who walked a different path: the outliers. The flamboyant hair, the radical clothing, the independent spirits, those were *her* people. And for a short time, she was actually happy, dating a lanky boy named Collin who wrote poetry and prided himself on fighting against the *zombies*, otherwise known as the 1 percent. Until her mother found out about it and made it crystal clear that she was having *none* of it.

"You are not going to ruin this family's reputation by hanging out with street rats." And Cecilia meant it, even going as far as sending Sophie away for an entire summer to a camp for troubled teens. *Troubled and entitled teens.* What a nightmare that turned out to be, the man in charge, ex-military.

From then on, Sophie watched her independent and free-spirited friends from a distance, laughing and being themselves, something her mother was determined to grind out of Sophie with a metal file.

And then she met Chad Lancaster, who, out of the blue, asked her to the junior prom. Good at sports and a star student, Chad was friends with everyone. Well, everyone who had money and influence—or could provide him with an A in whatever course he chose to take. He was handsome, he was charming, and he was determined to win over Sophie's heart. Six feet tall, Chad's light-brown hair framed his well-proportioned face beautifully, his clothes always coordinated and crisp, his smile bright. When he wasn't slamming balls on the high school tennis court or the golf course, he spent time with Sophie. And he smelled so goddamn nice, a blend of cedar, cardamon, and orange blossom.

He was so sure of himself, and maybe that was why Sophie had fallen for him. Chad complimented Sophie's sleek body, long black hair, and big hazel eyes on a regular basis. He often compared her to Mila Kunis, who Sophie believed was out of her league. It was a far cry from Gollum, and she appreciated the compliment.

Being with Chad bridged the Grand Canyon-sized gap between Sophie and the other kids, not to mention her mother. As long as she was with *him*, she was all right by them.

Thinking back, Sophie could see the red flags flew high. She just chose not to acknowledge or accept them for what they were. Like when Chad convinced her to go to a high school rager, where he drank way too much and disappeared for two hours. "*I passed out*" was his excuse, his normally perfect crop of hair tousled, his shirt buttoned wrong. They'd only been dating for a few weeks. Not enough time to lay down the law on infidelity. And then, in college, he became a little rough with her once or twice when she'd argued with him about politics in front of his friends, a subject she usually avoided, mainly because she disagreed with pretty much everything Chad had to say on the subject. But he apologized and continued to shower her with compliments and gifts, so she let it go. Over time, Chad talked about spicing things up in the bedroom. He bought new toys to try, watched raunchy videos with her, and even suggested they try a threesome. *"Everyone does three-somes, hon,"* he'd said. *"It'll be fun. We're young. This is our time to experiment, right?"*

*Everyone does threesomes?*

And being the obedient girlfriend that her mother had taught her to be, Sophie went along, not enjoying the experience one bit. She'd wondered if she had slunk out of the room during the event, if Chad and the big-breasted, blonde waitress Chad had recruited from Cooligans, a college bar in town, would have even noticed. But Sophie stayed. She cringed, and she dealt with it. She loved Chad and tried to give him what he wanted. At the time, she didn't feel she had much choice.

But the real warning signs sounded off like sirens the minute she said two words: "I do." And then everything changed.

"Enough," Sophie shouted at the soothing light-gray-colored walls of her living room. "Get your butt up and out for a walk." She hated the self-loathing. And although she'd spent seven unmarried years with that asshole (they'd married a year after college), it only took her six months after walking down the aisle to leave him. Some women, women whom she'd met at her job—women who couldn't see another way out—never left. And she had, despite her mother's rumblings about it.

With her sneakers on, workout top, and pants secured—a

light jacket tied around her waist—Sophie flung open the door to her cottage and stepped out into the April Virginia sunshine, the air refreshing her spirit, the birds singing a comforting melody. In the distance, the Blue Ridge Mountains stood proud and prominent, the trees sprouting new leaves for the summer. Flowers bloomed, the air warmed, and the pollen went berserk, coating everything in its path.

Sophie's cottage sat on five glorious acres of land, three of which expanded into a picturesque wooded area, giving her plenty of space to roam. The two-acre lawn was a lot for her to contend with, but she didn't have to worry about that. Charlie had it covered. And now he was nearby. Her mother's head gardener, Charlie, had retired from Richmond a few months ago to help care for his ailing wife, Ginny. Sophie helped him find a house in the not-so-distant Charlottesville area since they were driving to University of Virginia's (UVA) medical center on a regular basis. They'd found a lump in Ginny's breast, but not the kind that warranted chemotherapy. After the lumpectomy, she went through radiation and hormone therapy. And, thankfully, she didn't lose her hair, something Ginny stressed over. "*I don't want to look like an old man,*" she'd said with a slight curl of her lips and a sadness in her eyes.

Sophie even took Ginny to some of her treatments when Charlie had to attend the selling and closing of their small home in central Virginia. In truth, she liked knowing that Charlie and Ginny were close, people who felt more like family to her than her own.

Over the years, Charlie had put up with her high school friends when they came to hang by the pool and even dried her tears a few times when Cecilia was on the warpath. "*You've got to make your own path, Poppy,*" he'd said, placing a hand above her heart. "*You can't let other people decide who you are. That comes from within.*"

*Poppy.* When she was little, she'd discovered bubblegum. And man, oh man, did she like blowing bubbles. *Pop, pop, pop,* she sounded like a goddamn popcorn machine everywhere she went. Needless to say, "Poppy" seemed like an appropriate nickname to Charlie. Of course, Cecilia put a stop to that, too—the gum, not the nickname.

Charlie Walsh was old; he had a slight limp from a bad left hip, his hair was nearly gone, and his skin weathered. But he was and would always remain the nicest person she'd ever met, his wife, Ginny, running a close second. The elderly couple had one daughter named Justine, who had died from a rare heart condition just before she had reached twenty-one. Way too young. That was before Sophie's time. Even though her life was cut tragically short, Justine was lucky to have such caring parents.

To repay Sophie's kindness, Charlie offered to mow her lawn and even clear a nice path through the woods where she liked to walk, one that connected with an actual walking path for the small community of homes bordering her property. He also did handyman work whenever she needed it, helped her shovel out from the one winter storm to date, and took care of the place in the same manner he used to do with her childhood estate. He was old but meticulous, and her father rewarded him well, giving him a pension, which was unheard of in his profession. Any medical bills Ginny acquired, Johnathan took care of them. Sophie loved that about her dad. It seemed he had a soft spot for Charlie, just like Sophie did.

At first, Sophie had refused Charlie's offer. "You have Ginny to take care of."

Charlie just quirked his head and smiled, the way he always did when he saw something in her that no one else seemed to see: her heart. "I still have plenty of time to dote on Ginny. I'm already climbing the walls. And I need things to do." He flailed one hand in the air. "Heck, it was Ginny's idea. 'Get out of the damn house, old man, before you drive me to an early grave,'" he said, trying to mimic his wife's tone. "'Go help Sophie.'"

Sophie wasn't sure she believed him, but she agreed, happy for the chance to see more of him and to know that Charlie would take care of her yard.

As she strolled along the path in view of a few luxury homes, one of them planted high on the hill above her, she reflected on this.

That was until her phone vibrated in her jacket pocket, still tied around her waist. She pulled out her cell as the name "Bastard Chad" illuminated the tiny screen. She thought about letting the call go to voice mail but knew he'd just keep trying. He was like that.

Hissing through her teeth, she slid the green call button open. "I told you not to call me anymore. What do you want, *Chad?*" She said his name as though it landed like poison on her tongue.

"You know what I want. This bullshit ends now! Get your ass back here and return to being my wife."

# Chapter Three

S ophie's nostrils flared, the hand not holding her phone fisted and flailing. "How dare you … You have no right … I am *not* your property." She was so upset that she couldn't get out what she wanted to say: *You are a deranged asshole who takes pleasure in hurting women. Stay away from me, or I'll have you arrested.* She knew she couldn't really have him arrested. Not without hurting her parents' *precious* reputation. What would Cecilia do? Sophie knew the answer. She'd side with Chad. She wasn't sure about her father. He was much nicer to Sophie than her mother had ever been, but he kept his distance. Always had. Anytime Sophie and her father started to form a bond, somehow her mother intervened. Picking an argument with Johnathan would surely force him to storm off. She was always watching. Was she jealous? What kind of mother would be jealous of a daughter trying to connect with her dad?

"You became my property when you married me. Consider yourself lucky I'm a patient man."

*Patient? Is he serious?*

She wanted to scream and did inside of her head. To be

honest, she was just beginning to stand up to Chad. Even when she'd left, she did so when he wasn't around. She'd remained in his shadow for years, the dutiful spouse. But that all changed when he pushed things too far, nearly killing her.

Chad exhaled as though trying to regroup. "Look. Things have gotten blown out of proportion, dearest. Come home, and we can talk. Truth be told, I can't even remember why you left. But whatever the reason, let me make it up to you." His voice was light and airy, doing its best to hide the monster lurking within.

"You know exactly why I left, Chad. And I won't let you do that to me again."

His laugh, or more his snicker, ridiculed. "What in the hell are you talking about? What did I do to you? Other than being your husband. Forgive me for being unable to keep up with your mood swings."

Chad sounded so much like her mother. Did she coach him?

"I'm done playing around, dearest. I want you here by my side. If you didn't want this life with me, you should never have married me. But you did, so stop playin' around and get your ass back here before I have to start explaining to your father *and the board* why my wife has decided to run off to the mountains for some unknown reason."

Sophie's lower lip trembled, her heart unsure what to do.

Chad had a way of making her feel diminished and stupid. Like her problems were petty. Like she owed him just for marrying her.

"I can't come back right now. I need more time." She heard the wavering in her voice, and she hated it.

Another long exhale from Chad. "You are testing my patience here." He paused. "Your father is holding a meet-and-greet with some investors next week. I need you here to represent me *and* your family. I want to make a good impression."

*Of course you do.*

"Come to this event, and I promise I'll be on my best behavior. I'll even give you a little more time to do ... whatever it is that you're doing out there."

*You'll give me more time?*

That was how abusers worked. They made you feel loyal to them while they controlled your every move. Still, Sophie needed more time to figure out how to divorce this sicko, and having him off her back for a little longer would help.

"Fine. I'll come to the whatever-this-is, and then I'm leaving." Her stomach disagreed with her decision, letting her know it with several gut-wrenching cramps. She almost doubled over.

Chad waited an uncomfortable amount of time to respond. "I'll see you next week. I've already purchased a dress for you to wear. You'll find it in your walk-in closet, along with jewelry and shoes, *also* my gifts to you." He made a grumbling noise in his throat. "I expect you to act like my wife when you're here, Sophie. I don't want these investors to think our marriage is unstable ... or that *you* are unstable. *Don't* make me look bad."

Sophie loaded her voice with as much disdain as she could muster without gagging. "Don't worry, *honey*, I won't make you look bad. But you have to agree to stay away from me afterward. I won't be staying." She wanted to add, *and you can't make me,* but that sounded so juvenile.

"All right. I'll play along. For now." *Click.* The call disconnected.

She had so much more to say to that bastard. This was a man who had pushed her to the edge of her sanity. And for what, a cheap thrill? He was sick. Before she married him, she didn't know just how sick.

Sweat seeped from her pores like blood seeping from a

wound. Why did she agree to his terms? When was she going to be free of him? Deep down, she worried that it might never happen. "Argh," Sophie grunted and rubbed at her abdomen, her stomach knotting. "You son of a bitch. I hate you!" she yelled at the dead phone, her body doubled over. "I hate you with every fiber of my being. You are evil." If only she could say that to him. If only she could stand up to him for good. If only she could—

"Are you all right, miss?" The man's voice from behind her reverberated through her nervous system, nearly stopping her racing heart.

"Ahhhh!" She jumped up and back when she screamed. Whoever was standing behind her had just scared the crap out of her.

"No, no, no. It's okay. I just saw you were upset ... My bad ... I can go." The man behind her stammered. "I didn't mean to intrude."

In Sophie's periphery, he pivoted his body back and forth as though unsure whether to run away or stay and help.

Feeling totally embarrassed for being caught chastising an inanimate object, Sophie prepared her apology. If she were on her own property, she'd feel more justified about screaming like a crazy person at her phone, but she wasn't. She was on the community path that connected with several of the properties in the area, most of them worth millions, the ones with big windows and incredible views. If her mother could see her now, she'd roll her eyes and, with arms crossed over her chest, stare down her nose at Sophie for, once again, being a doofus.

"No, you're fine." Sophie finally turned and faced the man who looked like an axe murderer (although she didn't see an axe) or maybe one of those survivalists, judging by the way his long, scraggly brown hair spilled out from under his green baseball cap. The words "John Deere" were sewn into the fabric with what used to be yellow thread but was now smudged and grimy. Standing at six-foot, two inches tall, the man had a beard that was also long, its length uneven, like someone who couldn't care less about his appearance. It surprised her. Everyone in Sophie's world cared about nothing but.

His T-shirt outlined the shape of a robust chest and muscular arms. The brown shirt was either stained or dirty, and his tan pants were a durable canvas material. His Timberland boots had definitely seen better days. Everything about this man screamed danger, except for his voice and the vibe he was giving off. And for some unknown reason, Sophie wasn't scared. She knew all too well that you couldn't judge a book by its cover. Chad had proven that to her. *Is he on a construction crew for one of the mansions here?* That would make sense, considering these places went through remodels all the time.

*Stop staring and say something.*

"I was just ..." Words escaped her. *You were just what? Screaming "I hate you" at your phone?*

The man raised a calloused palm. "Miss. You don't owe me an explanation. I thought you were hurt by the way you were doubled over, is all. Didn't mean to startle ya." He spoke in a low voice, his head bowed slightly in a nonthreatening manner. He even backed away a step, his brown eyes wary.

Sophie exhaled, realizing she'd been holding her breath. "Oh, I understand now. No. I'm okay. I just got off the phone with my ... ex." She half-smirked. "Sorry you had to hear that. The man is an asshalf."

The stranger's brow bore down, his head tilted slightly. "Asshalf?"

"Yeah, it would take two of him to make an asshole."

First came a pause, and then the man unloaded with laughter. The portions of his cheeks, not rooted in hair, turned the color of watermelon, his brown eyes watering. He shook his head as he struggled to gain his composure, Sophie smiling proudly at her sense of humor. She made jokes all the time. It was just that no one had ever gotten them before. Until now.

"That's a good one, miss." He wagged a finger. "I'll have to remember that one. 'Asshalf,' ha." A few lingering giggles escaped his lips. "I've known a few of those myself. Asshalf," he repeated. The joke had taken hold of him, his entire face brightening.

Sophie couldn't help but wonder what he looked like styled, shaved, or even showered, for that matter. He had a pleasant aura about him and kind eyes. And after that stressful phone call, she was enjoying the reprieve.

She had truly tickled this guy.

He placed his hands on his hips and caught his breath as one would do after a hearty bout of laughter, his eyes shimmering with happy tears. "Man. It's been a long time since I've laughed like that." He took a breath as he wiped his eyes and ran a hand down his beard. "Phew. So you're okay, then? I won't keep you."

"Yes. I'm fine. Are you working at one of the houses here?" She gestured up the hill to where one such house peeked out from behind a thin layer of trees, three enormous decks framing the front. One extended toward the hill's edge, where it formed a circle for viewing, no doubt. She'd hiked up the hill once but only a short distance to get a better look. The enormous stone structure with expansive windows was amazing from what she could see. "I'm Sophie, by the way." *Should I have told him that?*

He extended his hand, which she took, his fingertips rough and lined with dirt or something dark. "Brian. Nice to meetcha."

She released his hand, which felt strong, his grip gentle.

"Yeah, I was hired to do some deck work for the dude who owns the house you've been staring at."

Suddenly self-conscious, Sophie lowered her gaze.

As if he could read her mind, Brian waved her off. "It's not a problem. Most people stop to take a gander at that place. A little too rich for my blood, but I know the owner. He and I go way back."

That seemed hard to believe. The owner was obviously a millionaire, yet Brian didn't look like he had two pennies to pinch. And then she thought of Charlie and the women she helped at her nonprofit job.

*Don't judge.*

Good people came in all sorts of packages. "That's cool. I've only seen the house from a distance. It's gorgeous. What does he do for a living?"

Brian's gaze drifted upward toward the impressive structure. "He dabbles in the arts. Been taking some time to himself. Doesn't like people around much. Except for me, I guess. But he knows me." Brian took off his hat and scratched his matted hair before returning it to the top of his head. "I probably shouldn't have said that." His cheeks flared a tint, his eyes full of regret.

Sophie made a noncommittal gesture with her hands. "Oh, it's fine. I won't say anything to anyone. I really don't know anyone around here anyway. Only an elderly couple who live in Charlottesville about thirty miles east of here."

"And the asshalf, I assume." Brian smirked, lifting his index finger for emphasis, his eyes shining with humor.

The man wasn't much to look at, but something about him was positively adorable, his eyes an interesting shade of brown she hadn't seen before. No flecks of amber or any other color, really, just straight brown like a chocolate river. She felt like she could talk to him for hours, and that wasn't something she experienced often. The only other people who made her feel that way were Charlie and Ginny.

"Well, lucky for me, the asshalf lives in Richmond, an hour-and-a-half away. We've been separated for six months."

"That sucks." Brian stroked his beard some more, which Sophie assumed was probably a habit.

With her hair pulled up in a ponytail, she liked to twirl the new strands growing at the back of her neck, which she just realized she was doing now. That was *her* habit. "Believe me, it sucked far worse living with him." And man did it. The thought of sharing a bed with that man made her skin crawl even now.

Brian drew his chin inward, his face alarmed. "Ouch."

Not wanting to come off like a complete bitch, Sophie tried to think of something else to say. "Yeah, well ..."

For a time, no one spoke.

Finally, Brian cleared his throat. "You work in the area?"

It was a fair question, considering Sophie had already quizzed him about his job. "Yeah, I telework for a nonprofit stationed in Richmond. I help young mothers or women trying to make a start on their own find jobs and housing." She stood a little taller when she said those words. It felt good to help people. It always had. And being around women who were unpretentious and appreciative was a refreshing change from her world, where everyone seemed to walk around with a stick up their ass.

Brian nodded. "That's cool." Then he noticed something. "What the?"

Something made a soft plunk on the ground in front of them.

Sophie stepped back to realize it was a small bird with barely any feathers, its pink skin all wrinkled and new. "Oh, no." She gazed up at the tall oak looming over them, zeroing in on a small nest perched on a lower branch. She pointed. "It must've fallen out of that nest."

Brian followed her gaze. "Oh, yeah. Shit." He crouched down to examine the tiny creature. "Looks like it's still alive." He stared up at the nest again. "I think if we can get it back in its nest, it may stand a chance." He stood and looked around as if trying to figure out what to do next. "I've got a ladder in the back of my truck. Do you mind staying here with the bird to make sure a hawk or a crow doesn't come snatch it up?"

*He wants to save the bird?* Okay, definitely *not* an axe murderer. "Yes, I'd be happy to." *Happy to?* "I mean, yes, go ahead. I'll wait here." She peered up the hill. "Is there an easy way to get up there?" The house was at least 100 feet away, and the climb was steep, from what she remembered.

"Yeah, there's a place just up ahead where I can hike up there, and then I'll slide the ladder down."

Sophie nodded as she sat on the ground next to the bird. "Okay, good luck. And let me know if you need help with the ladder." She held up her cell phone. "Should we exchange numbers in case you need to contact me?"

From his back pocket, Brian pulled out what appeared to be either an old phone or a burner.

That seemed to fit this guy's persona. He probably didn't even have a social media account, not for personal reasons anyway. "Go ahead." He waited while Sophie recited her cell phone number for him.

"Should you give me yours as well? Just in case?"

Brian scratched at his eyebrow, his eyes tentative.

Did he *not* want to give her his number? She couldn't help but feel a tad insulted by this. Then again, he struck her as an introvert. "I can delete it afterward if you want."

He made a dismissive gesture with his hand. "It's not a

problem." He gave her his cell number before he was off down the path and out of sight.

Sophie watched the tiny bird with a heavy heart. She looked up at the nest as several birds started to squawk from above, not the lighthearted melody she'd enjoyed earlier. It was as if they knew she was there and were not too pleased about it.

"Don't worry, little birdie. Brian is going to help get you back into your nest." She cooed as though she were speaking to a baby because she was. She wanted to pet the helpless animal or cradle it in her hands, but she didn't dare touch it for fear she could make things worse. *Plus, are you not supposed to touch birds or their mothers will abandon them?* She wasn't sure.

A gentle breeze bumped its way through the trees, inviting new leaves to rustle with their newfound strength. Sophie loved the sound of the wind in the trees. It had always comforted her in a peaceful sort of way. She hoped the little bird enjoyed it, too.

Meanwhile, the birds from above squawked louder as if in protest. *Get out of here, human; leave our baby alone!* The trouble was, leaving the bird wouldn't help either. As resourceful as they were, those birds wouldn't be able to pick it up and return it to the nest. Not on their own.

Sophie checked her phone. No calls or texts from Brian. She started a text to him, then deleted it. *Just wait.* He seemed jumpy about giving her his number, and she didn't want to scare him off. More time passed. She decided to hum, hoping to help soothe the bird *and* herself.

As she worried that Brian was never going to come back, the sound of metal rattled off in the distance, followed by a man carrying a step ladder walking toward her, dead leaves and dirt coating the side of his pants.

"Is it still alive?" he asked upon his arrival.

Subtle movements under the bird's skin told her it was.

"Yes. Did you bring gloves? I don't think we're supposed to touch it, right? Won't that upset the mother?"

Brian set the ladder up beneath the tall oak, his backside looking like he'd dragged half of the small mountain down with him. She wanted to brush it off but felt that was *way* too forward. Rubbing her hands down a stranger's ass had to be a definite no-no.

"That's a myth. I did bring a cloth, though, which should help." He bent down and, with careful hands, draped the cloth over the baby bird's back before edging it onto its stomach. The cloth provided a small hammock that Brian was able to lift and place into his palm.

With its eyes closed and skin devoid of feathers, the poor little thing looked weak and vulnerable.

By now, the birds above her were screaming. Sophie imagined a bunch of mothers distressed and yelling back and forth about what they were witnessing. Did they think they were going to dispose of their baby? That would be Sophie's guess.

"Do you hear that?" Sophie asked, gazing upward with trepidation.

"Uh, yup. Let's get this little guy ... or girl into its nest before they go ballistic and cover us in bird shit." He handed the bird wrapped in cloth over to Sophie. "Give it back to me when I get halfway up the ladder."

The noise grew louder, a cacophony of outrage as Brian climbed each step. "Okay, I'm ready." He leaned over.

Sophie did as he asked, the noise in the air almost unbearable. But when Brian gently placed the bird back into its nest and quickly descended the ladder, something amazing happened. Silence. Not a chirp permeated the air.

Brian folded the ladder up and came to stand next to Sophie. "There were a couple of other babies in there. Hopefully, the mother will come back soon."

"Wow, I guess they approve of what we did." Sophie looked around in amazement. She could feel their eyes upon her.

"I guess so." Brian put the ladder down and then did something totally unexpected. He leaned over and kissed Sophie, his hand braced against her lower back. It wasn't a passionate kiss, more of a tender, thank-you-for-helping-me kiss. No tongue, but not a peck, either. She expected rancid breath and BO, but his breath was fresh, his scent manly and not gross.

His hand remained firm on her lower back as Sophie's insides went a little nuts. She couldn't quite tell if she liked the kiss or loved it.

As though he'd come out of a trance, Brian stood back and almost rattled his head. "I'm sorry. I don't know why I did that. That was totally inappropriate. I better get back." He trudged back the way he came, his ladder in hand, his feet moving faster than they had during the bird emergency.

Sophie had kissed lots of guys in her young life, but something about this kiss was different. Very different. He wasn't a man who was trying to take advantage of her or someone hoping to get laid. Brian was thanking her. And she'd made him laugh. Something told her that that didn't happen often.

Now alone, Sophie stood there trying to discern what the hell had just happened, two of her fingers touching her lips. This man was *not* what she'd call handsome by any stretch of the imagination. So why did he just make her insides melt? *Maybe he was a mirage*, she giggled to herself.

She gazed up at the birds hidden in the trees. You all saw that, right?

# Chapter Four

Some people obsessed over reality shows. Sophie knew a few of them, her mother's chef being one. He enjoyed watching newbie chefs get their asses verbally kicked on TV. Others binged on a series through Netflix, Hulu, Disney, or one of any number of streaming services. Charlie loved the History Channel and anything pertaining to Nat Geo. Ginny preferred rom-coms. "*I like to see those handsome men with their shirts off,*" she'd say with a wink. Aside from reality shows that gave Sophie heartburn within five minutes, she could watch pretty much anything, but her go-to was *Entertainment News*, which mostly covered divorces and dysfunction within the confines of Hollywood's top celebs. Growing up as she did, she could relate to the dark side of privilege, which went hand in hand with her other guilty pleasure, true-crime podcasts. Both allowed her to multitask, as she was doing now.

She finished blow-drying her hair, then wrapped the cord around the hair dryer and put it in a drawer in her master bath. From her bedroom, just a few feet away, the TV blared loud enough that she could hear the latest news from the world of fame and fortune. While she listened to stories about new movies coming out and who was hooking up with whom, Sophie sat at her small vanity and worked on her makeup, her hands starting to tremble. For the past week, she'd been dreading this day when she had to make the trip to Richmond and face her sicko of a husband, not to mention a family that she felt about as close to as she did her mail carrier.

"Continuing our segment, 'Where in the world is Julian Sommers?' we tracked down his manager, Corey Fitzgerald, who was willing to grant *Entertainment News* an exclusive interview."

It sounded like the same reporter Sophie had watched last week covering the story.

Happy to think about something other than her drive of doom, Sophie pushed her stool back, bringing the TV mounted on the wall into full view. Yup, it was the same flawless reporter from before. The woman, who Sophie was sure had referred to herself as Lisa, sat across from a man with wavy hair that was mostly gray, pulled back into a ponytail, his clothing casual but probably designer. Rich people had a way of looking stylish no matter what they wore. Beanie caps, ripped jeans, it didn't matter.

"Hello, everyone. I'm Lisa Pantera, coming to you live from LA, where Julian Sommers's longtime friend and manager, Corey Fitzgerald, is about to grant me an interview about what has happened to this famous pop star everyone is wondering so much about." Lisa turned to Corey and crossed her lustrous dark legs, a small coffee table between the two of them. "Thank you for agreeing to this interview, Corey," the stunning reporter said with a beaming smile.

Leaning back in his chair with his legs extended forward in a casual way, Corey offered a subtle nod, his eyes tentative.

Lisa fidgeted in her seat as though preparing her inquiry.

"There is so much the public wants to know about what happened in that Vegas hotel room two years ago. Were you nearby when the altercation occurred?"

Corey sat up straighter in his seat. "No, Ma'am. I was covering a gig in Nashville that weekend." He shook his head and blew out a breath. "Crazy stuff."

Lisa nodded, her big brown eyes aimed at Corey. She batted her false eyelashes. "Yes, it certainly was. I can't imagine what that must've been like for poor Julian. And how tragic that an innocent bystander was also killed." Her face fell into a sorrowful frown that didn't look authentic to Sophie. "I've been covering this story since it broke, but sadly, I've been unable to track Julian down for an interview. I think his fans would like to know how he is. Would you be so kind as to give our viewers an update?"

Corey rubbed his jaw in a contemplative sort of way. "I have to be honest with you, Lisa. I haven't seen Julian in over a year. I've been busy with a new client about to break into the country music scene." His lips wiggled as if trying to hold back a smile. "You can expect an announcement soon about this young woman. Trust me when I tell you, she's the real deal, voice like an angel."

Lisa repositioned herself in her seat again, uncrossing her legs this time. "Yes, well, I hope that when that announcement comes, you'll give *Entertainment News* an exclusive." She paused. "But for now, what can you tell us about Julian's mental state? How is he coping?"

Corey tensed his brow. "The murder-suicide hit my man, Julian, pretty hard. I'm not gonna lie to ya. He reached out to the other victims' families, offering his support." Corey released a heavy sigh. "When something like this happens, it really makes you think. Julian made it clear he needed to back away from the public for a while. I've spoken to him a few times.

That's about it. Last I knew, he was doing fine. I suspect he'll emerge someday when he's had time enough to process things."

Either Julian's manager didn't know his client very well, or he was covering for him, unwilling to give out too much information.

"Well, please let our fallen star know that his fans are pulling for him, and *Entertainment News* would love an exclusive."

Sophie shut the TV off before the reporter wrapped up the interview. If she didn't hurry, she was going to be late. The trip was stressful enough, and she didn't need to add insult to injury, making her mother angry about her tardiness. Plus, she still had to stop at her house first. It was Chad's house now.

Fifteen minutes later, her car navigated the ramp for Interstate 64 east toward Richmond. She opened her window a crack to capture some spring air and to prevent her chest from overheating the rest of her body. It also helped her breathe a little easier. Fresh air had a way of doing that.

With her satellite radio blasting the latest pop music through the car's speakers, Sophie tried her best to avoid thinking about the last time she had been intimate with Chad, but it was no use. The memory was seared into her brain as though he'd branded her for life.

Before they were married, Chad encouraged a strange sex life, but she could deal with that. *After* they were married, his kinky tendencies turned more violent. Most of the time, they made love (if you wanted to call it that) with her bent over a chair or over the foot of their bed, his hand pushing against the back of her head until her face smashed into the mattress or the chair's cushion. Even that she could deal with until, once again, things took a turn.

They'd just come home from dinner with some of Chad's preppy friends, and they were both feeling the influence of several bottles of wine, Chad adding a scotch or two after dessert; Sophie couldn't quite remember. When they arrived home, she was feeling loose and ready for some fun with her hubby. She even flirted a little, teasing him with a short striptease.

With their clothes leading a trail to their bedroom, Chad slow danced with Sophie, making her feel special and sexy. He backed her up to the mattress, her knees buckling as she fell playfully onto their king-sized bed. Everything was going so well. And for the first time in a while—a long while—Sophie was starting to remember what she loved about her husband.

"I want to try something," he said, his eyes glowing with lustful thoughts, his breathing becoming labored.

When he hovered over her, Sophie put two of his fingers into her mouth and suckled them. "What are you going to do to me?" she asked in a seductive tone.

"Spread your legs, and you'll find out." His voice got all gravelly, the way it always did when he was in the mood.

Sophie expected toys to emerge, but none did. And then she worried that someone might be joining them, but no one came to the door. He was above her; she was below him. Everything was normal. *Was that what he wanted to try?* She'd thought to herself. As his hips thrust into her, he put his hand over her throat.

"I'm not going to hurt you. You have to trust me."

She did trust him, but then his grip tightened, her eyes going wide.

"Don't worry. You're gonna be fine. I need to fuck you like this." More thrusting, his grip on her throat growing increasingly more uncomfortable. And then he stopped talking altogether, his hips slamming now, his eyes glowing with unfettered rage or whatever was consuming him.

To Sophie, it was as if something had possessed him. "O-okay," she coughed out. "You're hurting my neck, and I c-can't breathe." She was terrified, like he was pushing her under the ground, where oxygen was scarce.

By then, his body was pounding into her as he tightened his grip yet again.

"Stop, C-chad. I c-can't breathe." Sophie started slapping at his hand, then clawing, trying to find a way to remove his grip. He was cutting off her oxygen. Was he going to kill her? Those thoughts and more spun through her mind as her chest burned for air. "P-please s-stop!"

But he didn't stop. The more Sophie scratched at his face, the more he seemed to enjoy the fight. She'd known him for eight years. Since they were kids, really. How could he do this to her?

Sophie went into full panic mode, her body doing its best to free itself from the beast choking the life out of her. She hadn't even begun to live. She didn't want to die. Not yet.

She wheezed, her pulse racing, her heart in spasm. She fought with everything in her, but Chad had the high ground, the weight of his body, his weapon. Faster, his hips rammed. Tighter, his grip squeezed. There was no way out, her muscles straining to protect.

Her life flashing before her eyes, Sophie wondered what her father would think. Would he care that she was gone? Would her mother? She gasped; she fought, but nothing helped. Her strength abandoned her, her mind losing consciousness, white dots everywhere. She cried, but no sound came out. This was it. It was over for her. She'd never accomplished anything in her young life. And now she'd never get the chance. What a horrible realization that was.

As the light went out behind her eyes, she swore she heard Chad say, "You little whore, you get what you deserve."

How long had she been out, Sophie wasn't sure. All she

knew was that one moment she was gone, and the next, she was gasping, her body springing up in bed, her hands flying to her throat. And not just her throat ached, either. It was as if Chad had treated her body like a battering ram, and she was sore beyond belief.

The sound of the shower trickled from the master bath. And then she heard him: Chad singing in the shower. He'd left her there, unconscious and nearly dead. And he was singing?

That night, Sophie slept on the couch, even though she should have left that damn house and never turned back. The next morning, she'd never seen Chad happier. Wearing a few pink welts on his face and hands (which he later covered up with concealer), he kissed her cheek as he made her breakfast. And then he said something that rocked her to her core: "You were amazing last night."

A horn beeped as Sophie realized she had been sitting at a stoplight just a few miles from a home that didn't feel like hers anymore. She was sweating, and her gut twisted into knots. Her hands shook as she gripped the steering wheel, trying to pull herself together. Using her left blinker, she turned onto her street.

That was one of the worst nights of her life, but somehow, when she met her mother for lunch two days later, she felt even worse. Sophie made sure to wear clothing that exposed her neck and the fingerprint bruises Chad had tattooed all over her skin. Cecilia had seen them. Sophie was certain of it. But she never said a word, just went on about some new drapes she'd found for her formal dining room.

Sophie wanted to bring it up herself, but she was too embarrassed. No. Too humiliated. This wasn't a stranger. This was her husband, someone whom her mother adored. How did Sophie feel? Worthless. Like her feelings didn't matter, nor her safety. If Chad had killed her, Cecilia would have believed it was an accident.

All she knew was that she had to get away from that deranged asshole. She would never put herself in a position where he could do that to her again. She'd go into hiding if she had to. Change her name.

As she unlocked the door to Chad's mini-mansion with a pillared front porch and an impressive fountain out front, she felt ill, like she was walking into a recurring nightmare. The vacant circular driveway brought hope that maybe Chad wasn't home. Maybe he'd already gone to her parents' house, punctual and ready to load on the bullshit for their investors. Or maybe his car was in one of the bays of their three-car garage.

Her bones rattling her from the inside out, Sophie passed through the foyer, her eyes scanning the formal living room to her right and then the dining room to her left. She honed her ears, listening for any movement within the house.

So far, so good.

Centering the room on a bench upstairs in her walk-in closet, a strapless, dark-blue floral ruffle gown flecked with gold metallic weaving awaited her arrival, a pair of four-inch light-gold strappy sandals, ready to complement her look. Chad had mentioned jewelry, but Sophie didn't spot any, so she went to work changing as quickly as possible.

Shoes on, she zipped the back of her dress up, ready to dart for the door.

"You look beautiful."

Chad's voice sent a lightning strike through Sophie's chest, and she jolted. She hadn't heard him coming.

He took a step closer, an impressive necklace held gently in his hands. "I bought you a present." He held up what appeared to be a tennis necklace studded with diamonds. "I thought it would look great on you."

Trembling from head to toe, Sophie wasn't sure what to do. She'd hoped to avoid this moment, gift or no gift.

"It's Tiffany." Chad approached Sophie, placing a soft kiss on her cheek, the palm of his hand running down her long, sleek black hair. "You really look amazing. I knew that dress would work." His gaze traveled down her body and back to meet her large hazel eyes. He took her hand and led her over to the bench. "Have a seat, and I'll put it on you."

On the outside, Sophie held it together while her insides were experiencing a three-alarm fire. Still, she did as he asked. She sat in front of him and let him place the expensive necklace around her neck. Every time his fingers grazed her skin, it crawled, her insides revolting. At one point, Sophie was sure she was going to vomit.

When he finished, Chad leaned closer and kissed her neck, the same neck he had tried so very hard to strangle the life out of. "I'm so glad you're here, Sophie. It's good to have you back."

Sophie rose so abruptly that she bonked her shoulder against Chad's chin. "I'm not back, Chad." She touched the necklace, the pads of her fingers admiring the cut of the diamonds. "Not after what you did to me."

Chad repositioned himself at the wide entrance to her closet, his body leaning against the door casing. He crossed his arms as if ready to hear her out. "What exactly did I do to you, dearest? What is this really all about?"

Sophie took a deep breath. *For once in your life, goddamn it, be strong.* "You know what you did, Chad. You nearly killed me. How can you stand there and act as though nothing happened?"

Chad smirked, his expression demeaning. "I didn't nearly kill you, dearest. Not even close. I was just trying to spice things up a little. To be honest, I thought you'd like it. *You* said you were okay with it."

Sweat dampened Sophie's armpits and chest. Even her upper lip beaded. "You thought I'd like being choked to death while you fucked the shit out of me? If you really think that, you don't know me at all. My neck was sore for days. I had bruises." She backed away and crossed her arms over her chest, but for a different reason than Chad had done. She was trying to keep the trembling in her muscles less obvious. She didn't want him to know just how scared she was at that moment.

"Whenever I've tried new things, you've never spoken up about it before. I'm sorry if I hurt you. It was unintentional."

The apathy in his tone told Sophie he didn't give a rat's ass about her feelings or her physical pain.

"*If* you hurt me? You *know* you hurt me. And I told you to stop. What did you think was happening when I was fighting against you? I never said anything about the strange toys or people you've invited into our bedroom"—she pointed at the floor for emphasis—"but I'm speaking up now! I never liked any of it. I just wanted a normal relationship with my husband. I went along to make *you* happy, but it's never enough for you. You always want more. And it took you nearly killing me to realize that fact."

Chad pulled away from the door casing, his hand patting the air. "Now, let's not get overdramatic here, dearest. I didn't nearly kill you. You were fine." He widened his stance, his shoulders back—a definite power move. "I didn't choke you. You're remembering things wrong. Like you always do. We had a lot to drink that night. It's understandable."

When Chad took another step in her direction, Sophie raised her palm like a stop sign, her hand starting to tremble. "Don't come any closer. And you can stop gaslighting me. I know exactly what happened. I woke up, and you were in the shower singing." She waved a hand in the air. "You left me there unconscious, and you were *singing* in the shower."

Chad's brow tensed, his eyes losing patience. "You passed out after we made love. I don't know why you're making this story up, but it's not true." He checked the Rolex wrapped around his wrist. "We need to get going. We can talk about this later."

"There is nothing left to talk about. After the party, I'm going home."

"You are home! The home you spent my money decorating, remember?"

"*Your* money? And it's not my home anymore." All Sophie wanted to do was run out of there. She felt so trapped, her heart racing, her mind spinning out of control. They were alone, just like before. A bad fall down the stairs would give Chad all he needed to play the grieving widower. He was sick, but was he capable of murder?

Sophie had to slow down her breathing. She couldn't faint. Not here. Not with him in charge of her safety.

With his index finger and thumb gripping the bridge of his nose, Chad exhaled. Loudly. "Fine." He lifted his gaze to lock with Sophie's. "But I expect good behavior out of you tonight. These are important people."

Allowing her pulse to slow, Sophie repeated him, trying not to reveal the terror brewing in her veins. "Fine." Feeling as though she were walking on a pair of stilts instead of four-inch heels, she maneuvered around Chad, and she was just about free when he grabbed her upper arm and hard.

"I'll give you a little more time to get your shit together, dearest, but make no mistake, I *will* expect you back here very soon where you belong. I tolerated you buying that cottage, even though I *knew* it was a waste of money. I've allowed you to work at that so-called job of yours, and I've put up with your mood swings for long enough. You are my wife, and I expect you to behave like it." His breath felt like flames against her neck, his cologne stabbing her nostrils with its pungent odor. She used to love that scent. Now, she abhorred it.

"Let go of me, Chad. You're hurting my arm." She refused to cry, even though her heart was whimpering.

Just like before, he didn't let go. He just stood there, his face inches from hers, his jaw clenched.

She could feel his bluish-green eyes boring into her. Adrenaline coursed through her body like water through a fire hose. *What is he waiting for?* And then it dawned on her. He wanted her to agree to his rules. No way. She refused to do it, scared or not scared. Not this time. She'd gone along for too many years already.

She yanked her arm free and spoke through gritted teeth. "I said, 'Let go of me.' Unless you want to explain how these *new* bruises got there, *dearest.*"

Unleashed, he grabbed her shoulders and slammed her up against the edge of the doorway, nearly taking her breath away, a searing pain traveling down her spine. "Don't fuck with me, Sophie. I've worked too hard to get where I am, and I won't let you ruin this for me." To punctuate his words, he mashed his lips against hers, smearing her lipstick and hurting her jaw.

To Sophie, it felt like the kiss of death. She never used to think that was possible. And maybe it wasn't. But he did want her scared. That was obvious.

Mission accomplished.

She pushed him back and ran out of their master suite. Holding onto the banister for dear life, she navigated the stairs, trying not to fall and break her neck. Once her feet touched solid ground, she flew through the foyer, flung the front door open, and sprinted toward her car. She'd already left her purse there in case she needed to make a quick exit. At least that was good thinking. The clothes she'd left behind would have to remain there. They weren't worth the trouble.

She spent the ten-minute drive to her parents' house calming her nerves. She was free, which she reminded herself over and over again. And she would never go back to that house again. Not by herself.

The adrenaline had subsided, leaving her mind to wander, which it did for the next three hours as Sophie dragged herself through the party of strangers, smiling and making small talk, while her mother did the same, only with a lot more enthusiasm and flair. Sophie felt like a ship lost at sea, with no sanctuary in sight. And no lifesaver, either.

Carrying large trays of various appetizers and drinks, uniformed waitstaff did their best to remain invisible while taking care of their guests' every need.

Everyone dressed in formal attire, including gowns and expensive jewelry. The women looked plastic, the men arrogant. At least, that was how Sophie saw them.

A small orchestra played off to the left, utilizing the Quinns' baby grand, its backdrop a set of enormous Palladian windows that overlooked a large patio with statues and more guests mingling under the springtime moon. Chandeliers cast soft lighting over human-sized vases, each brimming with flowers and greenery. They'd decked out the place for royalty.

When they weren't mingling with the masses, her father and Chad took several groups of men and women into other rooms to discuss business.

And then, after several rounds of heavy hors d'oeuvres and drinks had filled everyone's belly, her father insisted the four of them stand at the head of the room. He hushed the orchestra and then grabbed a wireless microphone.

"I want to thank you all for coming tonight." He draped his arm over Cecilia's shoulders and smiled, which she returned, presenting themselves as the perfect couple. "I see a great future for Quinn Investments. And with some of you onboard,

I don't see how we can lose. Don't be surprised when money is overflowing from your pockets because that is precisely what is coming. After tonight, I am more confident than ever. We've only just begun, my friends. Sit back and enjoy the ride. Quinn Investments is about to take this country by storm." He leaned forward and gazed over at Sophie and Chad, who stood uncomfortably close for Sophie's taste. "And who knows, maybe someday we'll be calling it Quinn Family Investments, depending on how soon my daughter can give me some grandsons." He chuckled, as did the guests. "Or daughters."

Sophie cringed.

Chad slid his arm across Sophie's lower back and hooked her waist with his hand. "We'll do our best. Won't we, dearest?" He nudged her with the side of his body.

Sophie smiled and nodded; at least, she thought she had, but there was no way she was ever going to have a child with this man.

"Maybe we can start on that tonight," Chad whispered in her ear as if oblivious to the state of their marriage.

To Sophie, it felt as if she were sinking in quicksand. She never should have married Chad. She never should have let her mother dictate her life and her decisions. That would end now.

"Not a chance, honey." She beamed a smile, knowing no one could hear her, no one except Chad, who pinched her waist in response. More pain. With finesse and grace, she reached down and removed his pinching hand, held it for a moment, and then darted away toward the bar when the crowd started to dissipate.

Her father caught up to her when she was ordering a coffee to go. "Coffee? I'm not used to seeing *that* from my daughter, the party queen."

A tall man with broad shoulders, Johnathan was handsome, his salt-and-pepper hair always styled, his smile always bright.

Distinguished. His blue eyes reflected warmth to his well-proportioned face. He'd always been extremely handsome ... but equally elusive.

"Dad, that was a long time ago. I don't party like that anymore."

When he didn't respond to her remark, she pivoted her focus from the cup of coffee in her hand to her father, who was staring at her with such adoring eyes. He did that every now and then, but it had been a while.

"*What?*" Sophie fidgeted a little, uncomfortable with his limited affection.

"Just admiring my daughter. You have turned into such a beautiful woman, Sophie. I hope you know that." His eyes grew sad. "I know I haven't been—"

"Johnathan, your guests are leaving. Shouldn't we be at the door right now?" Cecilia shoved her way in between them.

Sophie expected as much. "That's okay, Dad. I've gotta long drive anyway."

Johnathan tensed his brow. "You're not staying at home tonight? Chad said you were home for a while. And how long is that job going to keep you away from here? It's been over six months already. How are you supposed to give me any grandkids when you're never around?"

Yup, her father knew nothing about her marital troubles. And apparently, Chad had given him some bullshit story about why she had been away. Speaking of the devil himself, Chad appeared. "Why don't you go and say goodbye to your guests, Johnathan? I'll walk my lovely wife out."

With her hand already laced firmly inside the crook of Johnathan's arm, Cecilia escorted her husband away, never looking back at her daughter. She had maybe said two words to Sophie all evening. "Nice dress" was pretty much all that Cecilia could muster. And that was probably because she assumed Chad had purchased it. Honestly, it was as if she and Chad were teaming up with each other.

Sophie always suspected this.

Once again, Sophie was stuck with Chad. "I don't need an escort to my car. Thanks, anyway."

Not taking no for an answer, Chad took hold of Sophie's free arm like he had done to her at their house. He leaned in. "You know our deal. The night isn't over yet. I expect smiles from you until you're gone. And we aren't finished with our earlier conversation."

Sophie whisper-shouted back. "Let go of me, or I will make a scene. I'm not playin'. You've put your grubby hands on me for the last time." And she meant it. His behavior was getting worse by the hour. "Unless you want me to tell my father why I'm really out in the mountains. If you want to keep this charade going, you're better off without me here. That way, you can tell all the lies you want." *Did I really just say that?* Where was her courage coming from?

Chad smirked. "You think you're any match for me? Go back to your shack and hide. Enjoy it while it lasts." He turned, his expression bright. "Mr. Fredrick, Mrs. Fredrick, don't you two look stunning tonight. I haven't had a chance to speak with you all evening ..." And then he was gone.

When Sophie reached the highway, rain fell from the sky, a spring storm moving in. It was dark, the rain causing the headlights on the highway to glare and the visibility to weaken. Unwanted grandkids, strangled bodies, and Chad—untouchable Chad—basking in it all flashed through Sophie's brain like the veins of lightning scattering across the sky above.

At first, Sophie was angry, punching her steering wheel until she feared she'd ignite the airbag, and then she cried, despair taking over. It seemed the weather matched her outlook on life. With no siblings and parents who barely knew her,

Sophie felt so alone. Except for Charlie and Ginny. She had them. She even contemplated stopping by their place on her way through Charlottesville, but given Sophie's state of mind, and Ginny's health condition, she didn't want to alarm them. For now, Charlie's profound advice would have to do. *"You can't let other people decide who you are. That comes from within." I'm trying, Charlie.*

Would her father support her divorce? She knew her mother wouldn't. She'd be outraged.

Feeling defeated, Sophie pulled off the ramp and onto Highway 151 in the small town of Crozet. When she reached the roundabout, she took the second exit toward Nellysford, where her cottage awaited. Only traffic stood still about five miles down the road, some sort of accident, according to her GPS.

"Great."

For the next ten minutes, Sophie moved at a snail's pace, red brake lights illuminating in front of her. She came upon a lefthand turn that wasn't the one she would normally take but would get her to the cottage via a detour over a small mountain.

And so she took the alternate route, not entirely sure she was making the right choice. Two miles into her journey, the road turned to dirt, the ride bumpy.

Rain continued to fall, the sky lighting up before thunder boomed moments later as Sophie's thoughts consumed her. It was clear that Chad was losing his patience. And it was also clear that he would never own up to his behavior. It wasn't as if she could press charges. It would be his word against hers, and she had no evidence. She should have taken pics of the bruises. *Live and learn.* Back then, she didn't want to accept reality. And she was used to portraying a pristine image of her life. That's what her mother wanted. Until she left, Sophie was acting like a Stepford Wife. She hated that person. Everyone was happy, except for her.

Her dad thought so highly of Chad, enough to make him a VP in his firm. But if Sophie went to Johnathan and told him the truth, would he care? There were moments between them, like earlier at the bar, when she felt something stirring within him. Was it fatherly love? Guilt?

Sophie shook those thoughts from her mind. She was getting ahead of herself. She hadn't even called a lawyer yet. *What are you waiting for? If you don't get something started, you're going to lose!*

*Bang!* Sophie's car weaved all over the dirt road. At first, she thought a pothole had caused the unsteadiness in her steering, but she soon discovered it was worse than that. Feeling as if she were riding on a railroad bed, Sophie bounced around inside of her car until she pulled over near a guardrail to evaluate the problem.

Standing in the pouring rain, she stared down at a flat tire on the front driver's side.

"Shit." Having no idea how to change a flat, Sophie looked around her surroundings, which were nearly impossible to see through the darkness and the rain. She got back into her car and checked her GPS.

"Three miles to the cottage," she said to herself. "I can walk three miles. As long as I don't get run over by a car that can't see me or fall down a ditch, that is. Or be eaten by a bear." Man, it felt as if bad luck had followed Sophie everywhere she went. At least there wasn't any damage to her car. She'd done a good job navigating it off to the side. In the morning, she could call for roadside assistance.

If only the rain would let up. She peered down at her gown and four-inch heels. *This should be interesting. How bad would it be just to sleep here?*

A pair of headlights grew larger as the sound of a truck's engine approached. Sophie turned her head, wondering whether or not she should jump out and flag the driver down. She was on a remote road at the height of a storm. And she was three miles from home, wearing nothing but heels on her feet. Still, as the truck's engine pulled up and stopped, she worried about who could be driving it. She didn't trust her own husband with her safety, much less a total stranger in the middle of nowhere.

The truck's door opened and then shut with a clunk.

*Please don't be an axe murderer ... please don't be an axe murderer ...*

# Chapter Five

Knuckles belonging to a dark figure wearing a hood tapped on Sophie's window. "Ma'am, you having some trouble?" The man pulled his head and shoulders back as if noticing her tire. Then he tapped again on the window. "Looks like you've got a flat."

Sophie sat there trying to decide what to do, rain drizzling down the glass. Why couldn't it have been a woman at her window and not a man. A big man if she was seeing him correctly. Statistically, women were much less likely to be axe murderers. *Maybe stop listening to true-crime podcasts?* They were messing with her brain. And she still needed help.

She pushed the button for her window to roll down. "Yes, it just happened. I was trying to avoid an accident on 151 and took this alternate route. But I must've hit a big pothole or something that caused the flat. I have to admit, I'm not used to driving on dirt roads."

Sophie looked up at the man wearing a hood, which he pulled down before he said, "Sophie?"

He bent closer.

Wait, she knew that voice. She focused her eyes, rain sprinkling her nose and cheeks. "Brian?" Oh, thank God. The bird saver. "You kissed me." *Why the hell did you just say that?* "I mean. Thank you for stopping." Heat rode up her neck and face.

His long hair soaking up the rain, Brian smirked. "No problem. Not a good night for a flat." He glanced up, his eyelashes batting away the torrent. "You got a spare?" Straightening his posture, he backed away so Sophie could open her door.

"I think I've got one in the trunk. Do you know how to change a tire?" She got out, the rain pattering her gown and shoes.

"Wow." Brian's brow shot up, his eyes round and expanding. "Great dress." He scratched his furry chin.

Sophie stared down at her attire. "Thanks. I just came from a party my family was hosting in Richmond."

In an instant, Brian's jacket surrounded her chilled shoulders. She hadn't even seen him take it off. Scents of wood chips and pine coated the fabric. Not a bad smell. He wore a flannel shirt underneath.

"You must be freezing," he said.

For most of her drive, she'd been the opposite, stress-sweating over Chad and what to do about him. But the detour and the weather provided a distraction, returning Sophie's body temperature to normal and, with the drenching rain, below normal.

The sky lit up like the Fourth of July, casting nighttime light onto the sodden landscape. Two seconds later (Sophie had counted), thunder cracked overhead. Sophie and Brian both flinched.

"Why don't you stay in your car. You're going to ruin your dress and your shoes. Pop your trunk, and I'll see what you've got."

Happy to oblige, Sophie did as he asked, her cloaked shoulders grateful for the jacket and the warmth that came with it.

Another flash made Sophie cringe as thunder rode its coattails, then another, the duo wreaking havoc in the nighttime sky.

The storm was getting closer.

Not thirty seconds passed before Brian was at her door again, which she'd left open for him, water soaking the inside of her door and car. "I see the spare." The latest clap of thunder drowned out his voice, which sounded like lightning had hit a tree or a house nearby.

"This is crazy. We can't do this now. The storm is right overhead. I live three miles from here. Can you give me a lift home? I'll call for roadside assistance in the morning."

Emphasizing her words, the sky bellowed down from above.

*Boom* sounded from the sky. And then another one. The flashes made Sophie think of a celebrity walking down the red carpet, camera flashes everywhere.

Brian shouted over the din. "Sure thing. Grab what you need, and lock your car. It should be fine here overnight. This road doesn't get much traffic, and you're pulled over to the side."

After unstrapping her heels, Sophie grabbed her purse and shoes and darted toward Brian's truck, locking her doors with her key fob.

Water sloshed around her ankles, a few stones shooting pain through the pads of her feet.

She flung the heavy metal door to Brian's truck open and jumped inside. The truck's cabin carried the same woody fragrance that engulfed Brian's clothing.

In some ways, she preferred his scent to an expensive bottle from a department store. It made her think of that horrible summer camp Cecilia had made her attend, the one for entitled kids, but in a good way. She recalled the smell of the cabin she'd stayed in by the lake and the conifers crowding the woods as she strolled through. Nature—that's what it made her think of. And if Sophie pardoned her own pun, his scent was *growing* on her.

Realizing her strapless dress was creeping a tad too low, she pulled it up and glanced over at Brian, who had already noticed, judging by the direction of his gaze. When she caught him staring, he sat back in his seat and cleared his throat. "I'm glad I happened by when I did. Hate to think of you hoofing it all the way home in that fancy getup of yours."

"Yeah, thank you. I'm glad you came along, too."

The rain glowed like crystals before Brian's headlights as he shifted the truck into drive and fed the engine gas. Soon, they were driving toward Sophie's place, albeit at a slow pace, the bumpy road tossing Sophie around in her seat like a mini trampoline.

"Must've been quite an event to warrant a dress like that one." Brian kept his eyes peeled on the road, but Sophie sensed he was paying a lot more attention to her than he let on.

Memories of the party and what happened beforehand with Chad stabbed at her heart. Her chest felt heavy, as if she were returning to her own private prison, the one Chad had locked her in. "Yeah, quite an event." She sounded about as enthused as the character Wednesday would from *The Addam's Family*.

"Was Asshalf there?" Brian asked in a timid voice.

"Oh, yeah. Asshalf was there. Who do you think bought the dress?" Suddenly, Sophie wanted to rip it from her body and toss it out the window into the stormy weather. Maybe run it over a few times with Brian's truck. "Take this next left." She pointed.

Brian navigated the turn. "Well, he may be an asshalf, but he's got good taste." He glanced over, a twinkle sparking in his dark-brown eyes. "And I'm not just talkin' about the dress." He paused, lifting one hand just above the steering wheel. "Don't worry. I'm not hitting on ya, although I can see why you might think so after that kiss."

Sophie was glad he'd brought up the kiss, although she wasn't sure how to counter. During the five-minute drive home, Chad had been consuming her thoughts. Again. "I'm the second turn on the right."

As he pulled his truck up her driveway, he mumbled. "Just stating the obvious."

She didn't mean to ignore Brian. But that was precisely what she was doing. *Chad, get out of my head!* "Thank you for the compliment. But trust me, it's the dress." She smiled at him. "Hard to look bad in something this nice." For years, Sophie had struggled with her self-image. She often wondered if her mother or Chad ever really *saw* her. They had a way of looking down at her as if she were a petulant child who required more attention than either of them wanted to provide. A flick of their hand. A roll of their eyes. She was their nuisance. As far as her father was concerned, his compliments were limited. Like a blue moon, they were rare.

Brian's voice lifted a little. "I think it has much more to do with the model wearing it."

She made a *pfft* through her lips. "Oh, I'm not a model." Could he see her blushing? How long had it been since a man had made her blush?

When they parked, he turned in his seat. "If you want, I can come by in the morning and help you change that tire."

Sophie stared through the rain at her darkened house. She felt low, and she didn't want to be alone. With the heater blasting, Brian's truck felt like their own private refuge. "Why did you kiss me, by the way?" She half-smirked, hoping to keep the mood playful.

Brian ran a hand down his beard as though buying more time before his answer. Finally, he sighed. "Truth be told, I don't know why I did that." He raised a palm. "I hope I didn't offend you."

Before he finished that sentence, Sophie was already shaking her head. "No, you just ... caught me by surprise." Man, had he. She had thought about that kiss. A lot. And those tender lips of his. Not to mention those strong hands that held her lower back. *Don't go there.*

A slight chuckle escaped from Brian's lips. "That makes two of us."

Something about Brian's gentle demeanor drew Sophie in. She loved talking to him. Their conversations were light and nonthreatening, something she could appreciate as of late. And then an idea came to mind. "You got a wife or someone waiting for you at home?"

Brian raised both brows. "Uh, not that I know of. Why?"

Sophie grabbed her purse from the seat beside her. "I've got some wine or coffee or bourbon inside. Would you like to come in and visit for a bit?" She winked. "Don't worry. I'm not hitting on you, either." Although the thought had crossed her mind. Somehow, Brian made her icy heart want to thaw. He made her feel pretty but more importantly, he made her feel respected. His careful gestures and his compliments beamed light into her spirit. No one had ever taken the time to consider her feelings. But somehow, she felt that Brian considered nothing but.

Brian gazed out his rain-soaked windshield for a few seconds. "I guess I could do that. Nothing else to do in this weather."

The two exited the vehicle and made their way over to

Sophie's front door, which luckily had a small front porch covering it.

Still wearing Brian's jacket, Sophie unlocked the door, and they stepped inside out of the rain. A chill hung in the air, making a small fire a necessity. It was easy enough. All Sophie had to do was flip a switch, which she did after she'd hung Brian's coat up on a hook by the door and placed her purse on a small table. She dropped her wet heels on a shoe tray by the door.

After he'd removed his work boots, Brian stood on the outskirts of the living room, watching her work. "That's handy. My boss has a few wood fireplaces in his home. Takes a bit longer to get things warmed up."

"Yeah, we had gas at my ... at Chad's house, but my parents' place has the real ones." Sophie brushed past him on her way toward the kitchen. "Let's see what there is to drink. What are you in the mood for on this rainy Saturday night?"

Brian turned and followed her in. "What kind of bourbon do you have?"

Sophie went to her liquor cabinet, sitting right above her wine fridge. She pulled out a bottle. "I'm not much of a bourbon drinker, but will this do?"

Brian approached and took the bottle from her hands, its amber liquid sloshing against the inner glass. "Willett ten-year-old straight bourbon?" He gazed up at her in disbelief. "Last I checked, this bottle cost over sixteen hundred dollars. Where did you get it?"

Sophie was clueless. "Well, I took a few bottles from my home back in Richmond. Chad's home. Asshalf likes to stock all sorts of expensive liquor." She tried to mask her sarcasm without much luck. She scrunched up her face. "You know, any chance to impress people." And then something occurred to her. "Wait. How do *you* know how much it costs?" For a moment, she held her breath. Mainly because she didn't mean it to come out that way. *How does a hillbilly like yourself even know about expensive bourbon?* He was a simple man, but even simple men could be connoisseurs of fine bourbon. More importantly, she liked having him there and hoped her unintentional insult wouldn't cause him to leave. She exhaled, her shoulders sagging. Not cool of her. Sometimes, she could be such a bitch.

Instead of being insulted, Brian grinned. "Fair question. My boss." He shook his head subtly. "He's not really my boss. I'm doing some jobs for him. Deck and roof repair, replacing a few windows, and now he wants me to help him cut down some trees to clear his yard." Brian scratched his furry jaw again. He did that a lot. "Anyway, he's got a few bottles of the fine stuff around. Has a nice bar, actually. Just, no one ever sees it."

His boss sounded a bit strange, which sparked Sophie's curiosity. "Would you like a glass?" She took the bottle from Brian's hands and held it up slightly for emphasis.

"Yeah, I'll take a neat glass."

Sophie's browed furrowed. "A neat glass? I'm pretty sure they're all clean." She was dumbfounded.

"No water, no ice." Sliding his hands into the front pockets of his work pants (did the guy ever wear anything else?), Brian strolled around the cottage while Sophie poured him a *neat* glass of bourbon. Then she poured herself a glass of Veritas Red Star wine, her favorite red blend from a local winery.

"Nice place." Brian returned and took the glass from her hands. "Looks like you've remodeled?"

"Yeah, I've done a lot of work on the place." Sophie stood between the kitchen and the living room. She sighed, her gaze traveling the walls of her comfort zone. "I love it, though. It's nice having my own place. I've never lived alone before."

Standing next to her, Brian took a sip of his bourbon and smacked his lips. "Good stuff." Then he turned his attention toward Sophie. "Never lived alone, huh?" He seemed to size her up with his eyes. "I'm assuming a woman like yourself went to college?"

She nodded, her smirk egging him on.

"And let me guess. You met Asshalf either in college or high school and married right after graduation?"

*A year after, actually.* Sophie nodded again, her spirits dwindling, mainly because her life sounded so pathetic. Why didn't she live for a few years on her own? Chad, that was why. He was always in her life, always planning their future. By the time he'd asked her to marry him, she didn't feel like she had any other options. Being away from him and his manipulative ways, Sophie was starting to see things much clearer now.

Brian cleared his throat, bringing her back to the moment. "Didn't mean to bring up a touchy subject."

Sophie could see the concern in his eyes. She didn't want his pity. Deep down she didn't think she deserved it. She'd been with Asshalf for years. She'd endured many tense moments, sexually and otherwise. She should have left sooner. Or maybe stood on her own two feet and remained single. The thought had never occurred to her before. And how lame was that?

She put her glass of wine down on the kitchen island. "I need to change out of this dress. Make yourself comfortable on the sofa or by the fire, and I'll be right back." She made a quick exit.

After she'd changed into a coral-colored cashmere sweater, leggings, and a pair of fluffy socks, she sat at the end of her bed evaluating her life. She'd been doing that a lot lately. Maybe things would be different if Chad had simply said, "*I was wrong, forgive me. I love you. Please come home.*" But he didn't.

He wanted her there for appearances only. And what kind of man would abuse a woman sexually the way he had done with her? He'd crossed a line, and something told Sophie it would only get worse from here. Deep down, she questioned whether or not she even loved Chad. They were so very different.

"You okay in there?" Brian tapped on the outside of her bedroom door with his knuckles. "Uh, I probably should run."

Sophie stood and rushed to the door, thrusting it open. "No. Please stay. I'm sorry. I'd really like the company." She pleaded to his friendly eyes, hoping to convince him.

Where Chad made Sophie feel guarded and afraid, Brian had the opposite effect. When they'd saved the bird, they had worked as a team. When he'd helped her get home, he didn't criticize. *Why were you on this terrible road during a bad storm? Why weren't you watching where you were going with your tire?* She could hear her mother and Chad scolding her from within her mind. Brian didn't seem to care about any of that. He was happy to help the bird, and he was just as happy to help her. Simple as that. No complications. He didn't ask for anything in return.

She could also tell he thought she was attractive, but he was too much of a gentleman to overstep. When Chad took her to the junior prom, he'd practically mauled her. If she remembered correctly, he'd even torn her dress.

Brian's voice popped that unpleasant memory with a verbal pin. "You sure you want me to stay?"

"Yes, please stay. Where's your drink? Need a refill ...?"

The fire cast a warm glow over the living room as rain pattered the windows outside, light from the kitchen alleviating the need to turn on any additional lamps. With her legs curled under her butt, Sophie sat nestled in her oversized arm chair, a glass of red wine in her hands.

Stretched out on his side, Brian took to the floor, a well-padded carpet supporting his frame, his bourbon only inches away.

"So what's the deal with your boss? Or should I say your old friend? Is he one of those eccentric rich types who can't be around people?" Sophie knew a few of those.

Brian sat up and sipped his drink, the rain filling the silence between them. "I don't know if I should be talking about him. He's been through a lot."

Sophie waved a palm. "No worries. I totally understand. To be honest with you, Brian, I don't exactly have a crowd around me, either. I never made good friends." She shook her head in shame. "I let my mother and Asshalf dictate my social life." She took a breath and raised her chin in defiance. "Hoping to change that."

"That doesn't sound like too much fun. I'm sorry. Can't do much about the past, right? And you're on your own now, so that's something." He took another sip of his drink and then stretched back out on the floor, his body facing Sophie and the fire behind her.

"Yeah." Sophie stared off. *How long will it last?*

"Well"—Brian pulled in a deep breath—"I guess I can tell you. But you have to keep it between us." He made a motion with his hand to emphasize his request.

"Sounds juicy." Sophie let her grin fall away. And then she placed her hand over her heart. "I promise." She tasted her wine and then rested the stemless goblet on the side table next to her. She was intrigued.

Brian sat up again and positioned himself in front of her persimmon sofa, which he used as a backrest. "You ever heard of Julian Sommers?"

Releasing her feet from beneath her, Sophie sat up straighter. "Yeah. I watch *Entertainment News* all the time. I've been following a segment they're calling 'Where in the world is Julian Sommers?' Is he your friend?" She couldn't believe it.

Brian nodded. "Yup. So you know the story, then?"

"I know some of it, yeah. Is it true that a crazed fan killed herself in his hotel room? That's fucked up."

Brian made a face as if to imply what an understatement she'd made. "Doesn't get more fucked up than that. That crazed fan also murdered an innocent woman. She was lying right next to Julian when it happened." His posture stooped. "It's been a rough road for him. He blames himself for it all. Tried to reach out to both families involved. The suicide, I guess her name was Rebecca. Her family squeezed Julian for a few hundred *thousand* until he cut ties with them. The other family, the one of his companion, met with him a few times to find out what happened. They accepted his story but were devastated by it all from what Julian told me."

Sophie realized her mouth was gaping open and closed it. "Jesus. That's horrifying. Why did the girl do it? Was she batshit?" Sophie thought of those reports on *EN* and the stock photo she'd seen. *Those blue eyes.* Julian was gorgeous, no doubt, but most celebs were.

Brian's eyes widened for a brief moment. "From what he told me about her family, it wasn't a big surprise. They were what you'd call gold diggers, looking for a payout. Julian said they were the types that ignored each other's needs, always out for themselves. No matter the circumstance. Julian paid for the funeral, which was elaborate ... I guess. And then they wanted more money to start some sort of trust for their other child. Julian said he never met the boy. He said he always sensed Rebecca came from someplace like that. She was needy and delusional." Brian fanned his hands out. "I don't really know much else."

Still in a daze by it all, Sophie asked, "Wow. How is Julian doing now?" She sounded like the reporter.

"Uh, not great. Even though the chick was obviously fucked in the head, he still blames himself. He feels like he should have seen it coming. And if he had, the woman he was with that night would have been spared. Hard to reconcile that shit, you know?" Brian gazed up into Sophie's receptive eyes.

She brushed her silky black hair back, thinking about it all. "He shouldn't blame himself. There are a lot of crazy ass people in this world. And it's too bad Rebecca came from a messed-up family." (Sophie could relate to that part.) "But that doesn't excuse what she did. Not only that, Julian had no control over her actions. Until someone does something like that, there is no way to prepare for it or predict it. Look at all the mass shootings that occur. Everyone is caught off guard." Sophie couldn't help but notice how Brian's chin lowered, his eyes downcast.

He grabbed his glass from the floor and finished his drink. "That's what I keep tellin' the man. Not sure I'm gettin' through."

"I'm glad he has you, Brian. No one should be alone, especially when they're dealing with heavy stuff like that." She leaned over her lap. "When I first met you, I wasn't sure what to think of you." She clasped her hands together over her knees. "But you have a way about you that sets people at ease. At least that's how I feel, and I'm not one to trust people I don't know." She made a face. "Hell, I don't trust the people I *do* know. Just hang in there with him. He'll get through this. It takes time." She smiled. "I'm guessing Julian knows that. Otherwise, he wouldn't keep finding new jobs for you to handle. He likes having you around. I can see why."

Brian lifted his gaze, his expression brighter. "Well, I'm not so sure I'm the best company. But I do feel for the guy.

According to him, he made a lot of money in a short period of time. Sometimes I think he wishes he'd never been discovered. He told me he had become someone he didn't really like." Brian climbed to his feet and lightened his tone. "And that ... is just about enough talking about *that* subject."

Sophie stood, too. "Do you have to go so soon?" She looked at the clock on the wall, the hands zeroing in on midnight. *Man time flies.*

Brian stretched and yawned. "Yeah, Julian wants me there bright and early." He glanced at the window. "Looks like the rain stopped. What time would you like me to come by so we can change that tire? It doesn't have to be early. I'll tell Julian I need to run out for a minute. He won't mind. Shouldn't take long."

This guy was beyond nice. Sophie needed a few more of those in her life. Charlie would like him.

She walked Brian to the door, where he slid on his boots. "I can be up and ready to go anytime, so why don't you text me in the morning when you get a break. Oh, and don't forget your coat." Sophie grabbed it off the hook, handing it over to him.

Brian kept the jacket tight in his grasp. "Sounds like a plan."

Sophie placed her hand on the doorknob. "But I'll only let you change the tire if you agree to let me make you dinner to thank you."

He narrowed his eyes, a wrinkle forging across his forehead. "You sure you want more of *my* company?"

"Of course I do, silly." Sophie couldn't help but giggle.

His cheeks took on a rosy glow. "It's a deal, but next time, let's talk more about you."

That made Sophie gulp silently. "Or you. You haven't told me much about yourself, either."

Brian stroked his beard. He tipped his head at a slight angle. "That's because I'm not that interesting."

Sophie stopped herself from opening the door. "You're plenty interesting as far as I'm concerned." She didn't know why she said that. In fact, she didn't know why she wanted his company so much. Maybe she was just lonely. She'd spent her entire life with people either telling her what to do or controlling her every move.

Nope. That wasn't it.

There was something about Brian—and it wasn't his looks, clearly—but she couldn't get enough of him. And if she was willing to get real with herself, even his appearance was gaining ground. What was under all that facial hair? She was dying to know. His flannel shirt and canvas work pants did little to hide the firm body hidden beneath. *Okay, you can stop now.*

He blinked. "Thank you for saying that. That's very kind of you."

She waved him off. "Stop. I'm just being honest." Without thinking, Sophie placed the palm of her hand on his chest. She meant it as a friendly gesture, but it didn't feel that way.

A moment passed between them, something profound and heavy, both of them gazing into each other's eyes. Sophie wanted to look away, but she couldn't. He had entranced her. And when he leaned in for a kiss, she didn't pull away. She wanted his lips touching hers. Maybe mountain men were becoming her thing. It didn't hurt matters that this guy could kick Chad's ass six ways to Sunday.

When his lips were about to touch hers, Brian hesitated. "Is this okay? I didn't exactly ask you the last time."

Sophie offered him a slight nod, not sure what was happening between them or between her legs, for that matter. He'd fired her up sexually, something she never thought would happen again. If only she understood what it was about him that had caused her insides to tingle as they were. He wasn't what she would have normally looked for in a hookup—or even noticed in a social situation. Somehow, that made what she *did* feel all the more powerful. Less superficial.

Brian brushed his lips softly over hers, his breath a hint of caramel, oak, and vanilla from the bourbon. And then he kissed her for real this time.

Her hands combing through his long mane, Sophie returned his passion with her own, her tongue eager to interlock with his, which it did a moment later.

Was she cheating? *Who gives a shit.* She owed nothing to Chad. And they'd been separated for over six months.

Brian placed one of his strong hands on the small of her back, easing her body into his while his lips and tongue continued to tantalize. He applied the perfect amount of pressure, his tongue dancing around her mouth in a slow rhythm. He pulled back ever so slightly and then reengaged her mouth again, her insides melting like hot wax.

If he could kiss like this, what else could he do?

As the sexual heat between them grew stronger, Brian moved his hand up her back, his other hand taking hold of her jaw and then her neck.

In an instant, Sophie couldn't breathe. She gasped into his mouth and backed away, her lungs panting for air. It was as if a twister had set down in her house, her thoughts spinning into oblivion. Those hands she had welcomed just a few seconds ago scared the shit out of her now. What if he touched her again? What if he turned into Chad? That couldn't be possible. Yet the thought of it snapped around her neck like a bear trap.

Brian jerked his head back, his eyes as wide as an owl's. "What's happening?" He took hold of Sophie's arm, but she yanked it away.

"Let go of me." Bent over, Sophie lost all sense of time and space. Her body was spasming, her lungs paralyzed. If her heart beat any faster, it would explode.

"What did I do? I'm sorry ... I ... What can I do? Are you asthmatic? Do you need an inhaler?" Brian leaned over Sophie, his eyes trying to figure out how to help her.

It was too late. The bomb had already gone off inside of her brain. She straightened up, her head light, her knees weak. Her heart knew Brian wasn't a threat, but her brain wasn't listening. "No, that's not it. Please just go. I'll be fine."

Brian watched her, his eyes intense. He reached out to touch her shoulders but stopped himself.

Spots danced across her vision.

"Let's get you into the living room. You need to sit down. I'll get you some water."

"No!" Mustering all the strength her body would allow, Sophie reached over and thrust the front door wide open. "I said go! Get out! Now!" Feeling completely out of control, she shoved this gentle soul out the door as if he were yesterday's trash.

If he'd refused to leave, she wouldn't have been able to stop him. He was much bigger than her, but he didn't. He let her shove him out and into the damp night air.

"I'm sorry, Sophie."

She batted his words back at him when she slammed the door in his face. Gasping for oxygen, a feeling of claustrophobia invaded her senses, but she wasn't confined. Her lungs strained for every morsel of oxygen.

Was she dying? She wasn't sure.

Sophie slid down the wall, unable to do much else, until darkness finally pulled her under.

# Chapter Six

The rising sun welcomed Sophie's quaint little cottage to a new day, its golden rays sliding over the furniture and floor like the touch of a caring hand.

She awoke, disoriented, the side of her body stiff from the hard surface beneath her. *Where am I?* And then she remembered. The kiss. The horrifying moment that followed.

Pulling herself off the hardwood floor, she glanced out the nearest window, searching for Brian's truck. It wasn't there. She found her phone, hoping he'd sent her a text or five: *How are you feeling? When can I come by to fix the tire?* But he hadn't sent any texts. And he hadn't left any voice mails, either.

She didn't know Brian, but somehow, she understood him. He wasn't one to put himself out there easily. And she guessed he wasn't one to kiss strange women, either. She'd hurt him, and that tugged at her heart like a fishing hook. She knew what had happened between them was a big deal for him. And if she was being completely honest with herself, it was a big deal for her, too. Kissing had always been a means to an end: sex. At least, it always felt that way to Sophie. Chad had stopped kissing her all together, other than a peck on the cheek or that nasty kiss he had forced on her the night before.

What Brian did was different. His kisses spoke another language from the ones she was accustomed to hearing. His first kiss was thanking her. She was sure of it. She'd made him laugh. They'd saved the baby bird together. And he wanted her to know he appreciated how it had made him feel. The second kiss was making a connection. She could almost hear him asking, *Who are you? What is this thing between us? And are you willing to find out?* She'd answered him with an astounding yes. That was, until her body had some sort of seizure when he'd touched her neck. What was that all about? She couldn't control it, and she feared that if she didn't get him out of her home right away, things would have gotten worse. She didn't want to put him through that. She didn't want him to know what Chad had done to her. It had happened over six months ago, but last night, it all came flooding back, tormenting her all over again.

With unsteady fingers and messy hair, Sophie sent him a text: *I'm so sorry about last night. Please forgive me.*

She waited for the three dots, the ones that implied a response was imminent. None came.

After a very long and steamy shower, Sophie brushed her teeth and returned to the living room, her mood somber. It was Sunday morning. The sky wore a powder blue, and the birds chirped from the trees. The frisky mountain air rustled the leaves near her living room window.

She checked her phone for the umpteenth time: still no texts.

Biting her lower lip, she sent another one: *I feel terrible about what happened. I didn't mean it. It's too much to text, but I'd like to explain myself. Please text me back.*

No three dots, no nothing.

A large cup of coffee, some scrambled eggs, and toast gave Sophie the caffeine boost and sustenance her body required. She laced up her sneakers and went for a walk. The rain left behind a clear sky full of possibilities, nature enjoying the spontaneous bloom. Dodging around a few puddles, Sophie ventured into the woods where her property connected with the community walking path. Soon, she was where they'd saved the baby bird. "I hope you are doing well, little birdie," she called out, her eyes locating the impressive mansion on the hill. A hammer sounded off in the distance. Was that Brian? Or Julian? Or both of them working together? Her feet wanted to climb the hill and see, but her heart refused to relent. Flashes of her shoving Brian out the door, his face crestfallen, haunted her. What had she done? Would she ever get that chance with him again? Brian didn't strike her as someone who would take what happened between them lightly. He'd reached out to her, and she'd shut him down. Painfully. Did he think she was repulsed by him? *Beauty and the Beast.* If that described them, which role did she play?

When she returned from her walk, a flatbed truck was pulling out of her driveway. She flagged down the driver. "Hey, can I help you?"

The elderly man rolled his window down. "You the owner of the white Corolla hybrid?"

Sophie stood below the man's driver's side window, peering up. "Yeah, why?"

"Just delivered it. Put a new tire on it, too. You're all set." The man, with a few wisps of gray hair draped over his head and a scruffy jaw, attempted to roll his window back up.

"Wait. So you delivered my car and changed the tire?" Sophie lifted up on her tiptoes, hoping to find Brian in the passenger seat, which sat vacant.

"Yes, ma'am. As I said. Changed the tire and delivered it. Didn't have a key to drive it here." He coughed, his breath laced with old tobacco.

"Well, give me a minute, and I'll pay you."

The man raised a dirty palm. "Already been taken care of."

"By who?"

It was too late. The flatbed was pushing away.

It didn't matter, anyway. She knew who had paid. She just hoped it didn't cost too much. Brian didn't look like someone who had a lot of discretionary income.

Shoulders wilting, Sophie's arms hung like heavy logs at her sides as she stared at her Corolla. She'd loved that car. Just like her cottage, it was something that she'd bought for herself. It was modest, and it was perfect. Nothing like what her parents or Chad drove. In fact, whenever they gazed upon it, their eyes would roll, adding to her enjoyment. Her car burrowed under their rich skin like a tick, just like her outfits and her beliefs did. To Sophie, it represented independence. And her middle finger. She should have been elated to see it back. But somehow she felt worse.

Four days later—four very long days—Thursday arrived. Sophie gathered enough gumption to face the situation with Brian head-on. She was frustrated with herself and had to do something about it.

After work, she grabbed her keys and purse and made tracks. She had no clue how to find this house on the hill, but she was determined to figure it out.

Several wrong turns and two wrong houses later, she eventually found the one she was looking for, or she hoped. An impressive black iron gate stood arched at the entrance of the property, finials pointed, two stacked-stone pillars providing stability and strength. The gate morphed into an iron fence of the same design, only taller, that ran the property's perimeter. She'd noticed that previously when she'd attempted to climb the back hill to check the place out, even though she hadn't gotten far. That was before she knew Brian. Clearly, Julian didn't want visitors. And that was maybe why she thought she'd found the right place this time.

In the distance, a mansion loomed, its stonework impressive, its size generous. Various oaks and maples took root in the yard, obscuring the house while offering shade and beauty. *Are some of those trees the ones Brian is cutting down?* The sound of a chainsaw made her wonder.

She exited her car and walked along the pavers, finding a small speaker and intercom built into one of the stone pillars. Clearing her throat, Sophie called the house several times, hoping someone would answer. "Hi, my name is Sophie Quinn." She'd stopped thinking of herself as Sophie Lancaster over six months ago. "I'm a ... friend of Brian's. I was hoping to speak with him." No response came.

When the chainsaw silenced, she tried yelling. "Helloooo. Can anyone hear me? My name is Sophie Quinn. I'm here to see Brian."

And then she waited. And waited.

Startling her, the speaker crackled to life. "Hello?"

It wasn't Brian's voice. *Julian?*

Sophie couldn't help but feel a tad nervous. This was the elusive Julian Sommers, after all. The one who audiences screamed for. The one who women went crazy over. Literally. It was exciting to hear his voice. She'd never met a celebrity before. Yet the more dominant part of her couldn't care less.

The only thing she cared about was making things right with Brian.

"I said, 'Hello.' Is someone there?"

Sophie bent closer to the intercom. She pressed the "Speak" button as she had done before. "Is this Julian Sommers? My name is Sophie Quinn—"

"I'm not doing interviews *or* autographs anymore. Please leave before I have you escorted off my property. I don't know how you found me—"

"Oh, gosh, I didn't mean to." She stumbled over her words. "I'm a friend of Brian's. Is he here? Could I speak with him? I can wait out here. I'm sorry to disturb you. I ..." Her voice trailed off. This was a bad idea. She turned toward her car, ready to make a quick exit. Brian had clearly told her how much Julian needed privacy. And he had also told her how much he was struggling. Without meaning to, she'd just made matters worse. Surely, Brian would *never* speak to her now.

"Wait there. I'll send Brian out."

Outdoor voices carried past her ears. And then the sound of feet crunching through the yard grew louder.

His flannel shirt covered in wood shavings, Brian approached. His beard and hair had collected a few shavings of their own. Everything about him looked the same. Except for his eyes. Those deep-brown eyes carried an edge now. His jaw set as he stood on the other side of the unopened iron gate, brushing his hands together to expel more sawdust.

Still, he was a sight for sore eyes ... and sore hearts. Sophie's pulse ramped, and her palms turned clammy. When had he become, bar none, the most attractive man she'd ever seen? She had no idea. She just knew that he was. Part of her wanted to climb the fence and run into his arms. She had so much to say. Too much and, like a rock slide, it all came tumbling out at once. "Thank you for getting my car back to me. I need to reimburse you for the tow and the new tire. That was so nice of you." She hesitated. "I'm sorry about the other night. I—"

Brian raised a callous palm. "Look, I've got a lot of work to do today. And don't worry about paying me back. We're square. You shouldn't have come here. Julian doesn't like unannounced visitors."

But they weren't square. Sophie could feel the distance between them expanding. "Brian, I'm sorr—"

"Don't." He shook his head as if unwilling to listen. "You've clearly got issues, lady. And I don't have time for whatever bull-shit you're dishing out."

Sophie winced. *Did you just say that?*

The way his face hardened told her he had and that he meant every word. Okay, so maybe not a nice guy as she'd once thought.

Trying to keep herself from falling apart like a house of cards, she forced herself to hold in every emotion banging against her heart like a sledgehammer to get out. "I'm sorry you feel that way. And I am sorry about what happened the other night. It had nothing to do with you."

Brian widened his stance, his hands bracing his hips. "It sure felt like it had something to do with me. I never should have gone to your place. You got your car back. There's no need for us to continue talking with each other. Like I said, I don't have time for this bull—"

"Yeah, I heard you." Sophie nodded with angry eyes. "Good to know." Outraged and shaking from head to toe, she wagged her finger in the air. "I'll make sure I never bother you again." She blew out her lips in frustration. "You men are all the same." And here she was, worried that she'd hurt *his* feel-ings? He'd just destroyed hers.

What threaded through her thoughts like barbed wire was the fact that Brian was right. She did have issues—a total and utter fuckup. She wanted to blame Chad. She wanted to blame *someone*. Before common sense could stop her, she unloaded. "And even though you never bothered to ask me why I behaved that way, I'll tell you. I behaved that way because I was married to a monster. And now I'm scarred for life, *thank you very much*. Good luck with your work, and tell Julian sorry for the interruption. Now you know Julian's secrets *and* mine. You can take both of them to the grave, you fucking asshole." Livid, Sophie didn't wait for Brian to reply, and she didn't even look at him as she stormed over to her car, jumped in, and turned the vehicle around, her wheels carving a slight skid mark on the pavers as she raced off.

Tears ran down her cheeks like mini waterfalls. It had been a long time since she'd cried this much. Really cried, and so she did. With abandon. Why did she expect that Brian would be different? Men were all pigs. Self-centered dickheads who only cared about themselves.

Another thought cut away at her already depleted self-esteem. Had Chad turned her into a mental case? As Brian so eloquently pointed out, she had issues. "Yeah, no shit, Sherlock." *What did you expect would happen? You did scream in his face and physically shove him out of your house.* She was naive to think that since Brian had such compassion for his friend, Julian, he would extend that same courtesy to her. In all honesty, he didn't even know Sophie. And now he never would. She slammed her hand against the steering wheel before she decided what to do next. And then it came to her.

"I need wine. I need chocolate. And I need them now!"

* * *

Charlottesville provided Sophie with everything she needed. It took stopping at three stores, but she was satisfied with the results. While in town, she contemplated visiting Charlie and Ginny again, but she hadn't called ahead and didn't want to catch them at a bad moment. With Ginny's precarious health issues, they didn't need people popping in unannounced. Plus, they'd see right through her superficial smile and know something was wrong. She made a mental note to contact them soon.

With her cupboards stocked, she made herself a creamy chicken with spinach dish she'd found the recipe for online, a pot of rice to go with it. She lit a candle, poured herself a tall glass of red blend, and enjoyed her dinner for one while she surfed the net, mostly about stories pertaining to Julian and Rebecca, the crazed fan. She recalled how guarded Julian sounded on the gate's intercom. *Do not disturb.* He was trapped, and she could relate to that.

Before shutting her laptop down, she watched a few short videos of Julian on stage in his element. He looked so at home there, connecting with his fans as he traipsed back and forth across the stage, waving and riling up his audience, his T-shirt and jeans snug, his cowboy boots, sexy as hell. The camera zoomed in on his strong jawline and full lips, ready to belt out some lyrics. He had a cleft chin for heaven's sake.

In one video, he pulled an attractive young woman from the audience, guided her over to a set of stools, which sat center stage, and sang a song to her he called "Sunshine." Taking the stool next to her and resting his guitar on his lap, Julian sang his heart out as if this woman—probably a total stranger—were the most important person in his life. Sophie would bet that every woman in that arena wished she were up there, living the romantic dream. Julian was gorgeous—glacial blue eyes, his brown hair with caramel highlights styled perfectly imperfect. And Sophie couldn't help but feel a tad starstruck that she had actually spoken to the man. Albeit in a get-the-hell-out-of-here sort of way.

She also looked him up on every social media platform she could think of, but he wasn't on any of them. It wasn't a shocker, considering what he was going through.

She sat on her comfy sofa enjoying a gourmet chocolate bar while sipping her third glass of the night. With the TV muted, a story came on about Julian Sommers once again. *Did Entertainment News cover anything else?* Interest piqued, she turned the volume up to find the same reporter, Lisa Pantera, covering the story, the opening music for *Entertainment News* fading in the background.

A full-bodied man and woman sat across from Lisa this time. In addition to her floral dress, the woman wore heavy makeup as if to cover up her blotchy skin tone or adult acne, judging by the way the light shined on her face. Her hair fell in loose curls, the color a cross between red and orange. With dark-rimmed glasses resting on the bridge of his wide nose, the man had short hair and intense gray eyes. His button-down shirt was too small for his body causing the material to pucker.

Were they Julian's parents? They looked young. If they were, Sophie couldn't help but feel bad for them. To watch your son go from unknown to topping the charts to *toppling* into obscurity, must've been quite the chilling ride.

"Good evening. This is Lisa Pantera from *Entertainment News*, coming to you live from just outside of Jonesboro, Tennessee. As part of our segment 'Where in the world is Julian Sommers?' I'm here with Wendy and Clifford Abbott, the parents of Rebecca Abbott, the girl who took her own life in that infamous hotel room two years ago." Lisa turned to the couple, who Sophie guessed was in their mid to late thirties. "First of all, let me say that everyone here at *Entertainment News* wants to express how sorry we are for your loss. I can't imagine how hard this was for both of you. What a tragedy."

Wendy and Clifford nodded, Wendy clutching a tissue in

her hand that she used to dab her eyes, a few sniffles filling the void.

Wendy responded with a southern accent. "Yes, it's been very difficult for us."

Clifford nodded, his face strained. He leaned over his lap. "Been a damn nightmare. My baby girl meant the world to me." He shook his head, his eyes downcast.

Lisa blinked, her gaze soft and compassionate. "I can just imagine. I understand that Julian reached out to you. Is that true?"

"Sure did." Wendy played with the wad of tissue in her hand in a nervous sort of way. "Felt raaght bad about what happened to my daughter."

"As he should! Damn it." Clifford glared at his wife, who agreed with a timid nod.

Something about the way he spoke to his wife gave Sophie the impression he was domineering. And that turned her off *right away*.

"There are unconfirmed rumors that Julian helped your family financially. Is that also true?"

Sophie knew the answer. Brian had told her as much. It sounded like they'd bled him for several hundred thousand dollars. She could also tell by the way this couple behaved that they were sympathy seekers. People who took no responsibility for their actions but expected everyone to make things better for them. Was that what Rebecca was doing with Julian? Hoping he'd change her life?

"That's raaght." Wendy dabbed her eyes again, her arms and fingers swollen from too many extra pounds. "Man like him coulda helped my baby girl. Becca idolized Julian."

Clifford sat back in his seat as he flung one arm up. "Hell, the girl plastered her bedroom walls with posters of him. Wrote him letters, bought his merch, went to every concert he gave.

Christ, she even got a tramp stamp of his face right above her ass. You'da thought the girl had lost her damn marbles. She followed him everywhere. Smitten, she was." His drawl was heavy, his tone indignant.

The way the couple spoke, they acted as if it was Julian's fault that this girl had gone nuts over him. Forget Julian. Where were *they* when she needed them? From her research earlier, it didn't take Sophie long to discover that Rebecca had been arrested for prostitution several times when she was eighteen. She was also homeless and picked up for panhandling. She'd had a tough life. Sophie could understand how a girl like her could cling to fantasies about a celebrity such as Julian. She may have seen Julian as her way out of a life that had done nothing but shit all over her. If Julian sensed as much, he was probably guilt-ridden over the whole affair. He offered them money to appease his conscience, even though he'd done nothing wrong.

Wendy and Clifford cashed in on their daughter's despair.

*How pathetic.*

"So Julian offered his help to you, then?" Lisa asked in a delicate voice. "Financial help, that is?"

Wendy nodded once. "He done what's raaght."

"Yeah, *raaght* for you." Sophie rolled her eyes and clicked the TV off just as the sound of tires crunching against the pavement of her driveway reached her ears. A pair of headlights pierced the sidelights of her front door, halogen beams reaching into Sophie's living room with their long, luminous arms.

She glanced at the clock. "Who the hell is here at ten o'clock on a Thursday night?" She got up and tiptoed into the kitchen, flicking the light off. "It better not be you, Chad."

A knock sounded on the door just as the doorbell chimed.

If it was Chad, she wasn't answering. She'd just wait in her kitchen where he couldn't see her. She had a few blindspots already mapped out, her phone ready to call 911.

"Sophie, it's Brian. Open up."

Huh? Brian? What was *he* doing here? Her heart raced as a shiver ran, like a tiny mouse, down her spine. Was he here to finish telling her what a sick person she was? She had *issues*, after all, she thought to herself sarcastically.

Another knock. "Sophie. I know you're awake. I saw your light on."

*Shit.* The jig was up. Why was she hiding anyway? She had nothing to be ashamed of. Her feet rode that thought like a freight train all the way to her front door, where she flipped the deadbolt and thrust the door open.

"What are you doing here?" She stood there with her hand on her hip, ready for battle.

Only the battle never came. Instead, Brian placed both hands on the sides of her face and planted his lips against hers as if he had no other choice.

*WTF?*

Her lips had a mind of their own, returning his kiss of their own volition.

Fragrant with wood chips and pine pitch, he pulled back and stood before her, his eyes vulnerable, his shoulders slumped. "I'm sorry. You were right. I should have been more sensitive. I should have asked you what was wr—"

"Shut the hell up." She grabbed hold of his shirt and pulled him down for another kiss, his breath fresh and inviting, his essence more than she could bear. She couldn't get enough.

Being gentle, he removed his lips for a second time. "Now, I don't want to cause you to have that same reaction as before. Maybe we better talk a little?"

* * *

It was like déjà vu inside of Sophie's house, Brian stretched out on her living room floor, tipped up on his side to face her, and Sophie in her oversized chair, her feet tucked under her butt.

Since he'd passed on the bourbon she'd offered him, she poured her goblet of wine down the sink and filled a glass of water for them both, sensing the need to keep her wits about her. "Was Julian upset that I came by? I hope you apologized for me. I didn't mean to intrude."

Brian stroked his beard the way he always did. "He was fine. No worries. What I want to know is how you are? The minute you drove off, I realized what a dick I'd been. I had no right to speak to you that way. And I don't even know where it came from." He sat up against the couch like before, his cheeks the color of bubble gum. "I haven't kissed a woman in years, and I guess I worried that maybe I was just really bad at it." He spoke with his hands before letting them fall to his lap.

The two exchanged a look, a smile creeping across both of their faces. And then they both flung their heads back, laughter exploding from each of their lungs.

For several minutes, nothing but their cackles filled the room.

Tears spilling, Sophie tried to speak. "You thought." She laughed some more. "My reaction." She touched her chest for impact as she tried to catch her breath. "Was because you were a terrible kisser?"

Regaining his composure, Brian fanned both hands out. "Well, how the hell was I supposed to know?" His voice remained light and airy. "Like I said, it's been years."

Sophie pulled her feet out from under her and let them fall to the floor. Then she reached for a box of tissue on her side table, taking one and stretching her arm out for Brian to do the same. They both wiped the tears of laughter from their eyes.

And then something repeated in her head: *He hasn't kissed*

*a woman in years?* She was flattered. And she felt lucky that she got to be *that* woman. Brian was like a restaurant that no one knew about, one that served delectable food. The finest. He was her best-kept secret, and she didn't want to share him with anyone.

"So I'm sensing you forgive me, then?" Brian tipped his head in a thoughtful sort of way.

Sophie leaned over her lap. "Only if you forgive me."

"Done." Brian looked around the room, his brain working on something. "Do you, uh, want to talk about it?" He gazed up at her from under his brow.

"Oh, boy. That's a can of worms you don't want to open, Brian." She took a quick sip of her water. "Or *I* want to open."

When she met Brian's gaze, he was staring intently. "He hurt you, didn't he?"

Suddenly, the air in the room felt like a heavy blanket over Sophie's chest. Her grin washing away, she nodded. Up until now, no one had known or cared about her sorrows. Her misery cried out from inside of her chest, her heart begging for understanding. All those years she had put up with Chad and his abuse. It had changed her. She'd drawn inward. But sitting across from someone who opened her mind and her soul, she didn't want to be alone in this. For the first time in as long as she could remember, she wanted to lean on someone else for a change. Someone she could trust to help carry her burden.

The corners of Brian's mouth turned downward, his eyes narrow and angry. "Fucker." He shook his head. "You don't have to tell me what he did."

"He tried to strangle me when we were having sex." It just came out, and what a relief it was to tell him, tell someone. She'd been keeping that ugly secret to herself for months, stored up in her attic of torment like a box of mothballs.

Brian flew to his feet. "Did you call the police? Someone needs to throw his ass in jail. Do your parents know?"

Sophie rose slowly and patted the air. "Take it easy. No, I didn't call the police."

"But—"

"Wait." Sophie approached Brian, ready to unload her ugly past. "Let me explain ..."

# Chapter Seven

When Sophie finished, she wasn't sure what Brian was thinking. He listened with intent, his face cringing when she explained in more detail what Chad had done to her. They sat at her kitchen table, a cup of coffee in front of each of them. She told him everything, even how estranged she'd been from her parents, and how her mother loved Chad more than her.

"It wasn't all his fault. I did allow him to"—she made air quotes with her fingers—"experiment with me. I guess I wanted to make him happy. Maybe I gave him the wrong idea." She felt ashamed and dirty just speaking about it. Until she remembered one significant fact. "I told him to stop."

Brian's brow bore down, his grip on his coffee mug tightening enough that Sophie feared it would shatter. "That's bullshit. And you know it, Sophie. I may not have kissed a woman in a while, but I'm no saint, either. If you're choking your wife unconscious to get off, you've got serious fucking issues. I would never even consider doing that to a woman. Only a sick bastard would."

Sophie smirked. "He does have serious *fucking* issues. That's my point."

Judging by the two lightning bolts above each of his dark-brown eyes, Brian didn't see the humor in her off-color joke. "You can never go back to him. You know that, right? He could actually kill you next time."

Sophie shook her head almost violently. "I have no intention of going back to him. Ever." Just the thought made her stomach clench.

"Good. I'm sorry that your parents aren't there for you, but you still need to tell them. At least your dad. You said he's easier than your mom, right?"

"Yeah. I guess." Sophie slid her mug back and forth along the table's surface between her palms.

"And if he ever comes after you again, he'll have to go through me. I've never hit a man before, but he'll be the first. Trust me on that." Brian set his jaw. "I won't let him hurt you again."

Sophie couldn't believe her ears. No one had ever said that to her. Well, Charlie would, if he only knew. Her insides warmed up like a ray of sunshine.

Brian had broken through a dark cloud in her life, and she no longer felt alone. In the short time she'd known him, he'd come to mean more to Sophie than her own family. She wanted to run away with him, experience the world, and live. She didn't care that he was scruffy. She didn't care that he was poor. He had everything she needed. Plus, she had enough money for both of them.

"What's happening right now?" Brian's eyes narrowed with skepticism.

Sophie could only imagine the way she was looking at him. "I think I love you." She tried to pull it back, but it was too late. The invisible reins had snapped. She slid her chair back from the table and stood. "I'm sorry. I don't know why I said that. I couldn't possibly love you ... not so soon." She walked in circles, her head flustered, her hand over her mouth. "It's only been like two weeks. I'm being ridiculous." She hugged her waist and turned away from him, embarrassed and wide open.

Brian came up from behind her. His arms wrapped in flannel coiled around her, his chin resting over her head, his long beard mingling with her silken black hair. "You're not being ridiculous." He took a breath. "I don't know if you're really in love with me or if you're just feeling something deep between us. I feel it, too." He turned her around to face him. "I do. I can't explain it, either. It's never happened to me before."

Sophie leaned into her loving man, her forehead against his chest and all his wonderful fur. "It's never happened to me, either. I never felt this way with Chad ... or anyone." She pulled back and gazed into his receptive eyes. "Please tell me it's real." She felt so fragile and exposed.

Brian rubbed his strong hands around her back, his callouses catching on the delicate material of her velvet tunic. "It's as real as anything else in this messed-up world." He bent down to kiss her. "It's real to me." When he finished his next kiss, he ran his hand down her lustrous locks. "Goddamn, you are the most beautiful woman I have ever seen." He stared deep into Sophie's eyes. "I could get lost in those big, hazel eyes of yours. Any man who would abuse *you* is an asshole." A grin floated across his face. "Correction. An asshalf."

"Hahaha. Duly noted." Sophie appreciated the respite. She appreciated everything about Brian. Except for maybe his facial hair. That had to go. An argument for another day. Because on *this* day, she had other ideas in mind.

She slid her arms around his sturdy waist and looked up at him. "I don't know if I can make love to another man without freaking out, but if you're willing, I'd like to try. Just stay away from my neck."

Brian pulled away from her, his eyes startled, his mouth dropping open. "Do you think that's such a good idea?" He swiped a hand across his forehead. "Maybe you need to speak to someone, first, before you take a leap as big as that one." He started to stutter. "I-I want to, don't get me wrong. And I'd be lying if I said I hadn't thought about it ... like a gazillion times already. But I don't want to do anything that will set you back."

Ever since Chad had strangled Sophie unconscious, she'd taken a more daring approach with her life. Leaving him, which she considered One Giant Leap for Sophie-kind, was the first step. Buying the cottage and moving away, was the second. Life was short. And she'd spent too many years letting everyone around her manage her life. It was time she ended their reign.

"It may set me back. I don't know. But when it happened before, I was caught off guard." She thought about what it would be like to make love to a *real* man, her insides a flurry of sensations she couldn't quite describe. Her juices flowed. Her nipples hardened. "I don't know if what I feel for you is true love or not, but I do know that I want to find out. Do you?"

Brian exhaled, his eyes rolling around in exasperation. "Of course I do. Like I said, I've thought about it ... a lot." He chuckled.

A smile skated across Sophie's face, her aroused body edging closer to total and utter meltdown. "Oh, yeah? Thought about me, have you?" She reached up and ran her fingers through his long mane. "During those little fantasies of yours, what were you doing to me?" Her inner thighs trembled with anticipation.

Brian's eyes glowed in a way she hadn't witnessed before. "Well, for starters, I kissed my way down your neck, but since that's off-limits at the moment, I guess my next move would be to check out those great-looking tits of yours."

*Game on.*

Sophie pulled her long-sleeve tunic over her head before she unhooked her bra and threw it to the side. Her breasts were ready and waiting. "Go ahead. I dare ya."

Brian just stood there as if dumbfounded, a rather large tent rising beneath the fly of his work pants. He took hold of one of her ample breasts, his thumb grazing over her nipple, his eyes wide with desire. The guy was practically drooling.

Sophie let her head fall back, her breathing labored.

He cupped both of her breasts now, his lips inching down her chest until he suckled one, his beard tickling her stomach.

*What would that beard feel like between my legs?* she wondered, a moan escaping from her lips. Brian's hands retreated just before he swiftly picked her up into his strong arms and carried her toward the bedroom, where he gently placed her on the bed.

For the next few seconds, Sophie enjoyed watching Brian disrobe, first his shirt and then his pants, boxers, and socks. Just as she had imagined, muscles stacked his chest like bricks, his biceps the size of small melons. He was erect and ready for fun.

Sophie sat up and slid her leggings, socks, and panties off, feeling free and uninhibited.

"What's that?" She pointed to a large bandage covering Brian's left bicep.

Brian turned his attention toward the wound. "Oh, a branch caught me when I was clearing the yard. It's fine. Just a small cut. I've got it bandaged pretty well to keep it clean." And then his eyes scanned her naked body. "Wow. I have to admit, I'm a bit nervous here."

Sophie could tell by the way his cheeks flared that he meant it. She sat before him, taking his erection into her mouth.

As he slid himself in and out of her mouth, her lips caressed his shaft. Before long, Brian's head fell back, his hands resting on the top of her head. "Fuck, that feels good."

*Oh, yeah. I'll get you in the mood.* For several minutes, she did nothing but stroke him with her lips and tongue. Never before had she wanted to satisfy a man this much. Never before had she cared enough.

Brian looked down at her, his fingers running through her silky hair. "Let me take care of you now. I really want to." He eased her back onto the mattress as Chad's ugly face flashed before her.

"I don't want you on top," she said with a heavy breath. "Chad was on top when he ..."

Brian rose, still hovering but providing her a more comfortable space. "Copy that. Tell you what. You let me go down on you, and then you can be on top or wherever you want to be. You're in charge. Sound like a plan?" He waited with bated breath.

*I'm in charge.*

"Yes!" Opening her legs, Sophie closed her eyes and waited as Brian licked and kissed her stomach down to her inner thighs, his beard heightening her senses. When his tongue found her inner folds, she almost lost her mind. His tongue went to work, his facial fur adding insult to pleasurable injury, his fingers gently massaging everywhere his mouth wasn't.

She grabbed his head, anchoring him in place as her body quivered, her eyes rolling back. She had never felt anything like this before. The tingling, the intensity. *My God, she'd been missing out.* "Oh, please don't stop," she cried out and meant it. If he pulled away, she was sure she'd spontaneously combust.

"Relax. I'm just getting started."

And he was. Sensations rode her sexual organs like the waves of a tsunami. Only her wave grew stronger and stronger until her back arched and her lungs exploded, crying out, "Son of a bitch, I can't take any more of this." But she could take more, a lot more, as she soon found out. It was as if she were levitating, everything around her spinning into oblivion. Her body pulsed with sexual adrenaline, building toward its peak. And then she collapsed onto the bed, her mind a swirl of ecstasy. He didn't need toys. Nor did he need big-breasted strangers, either. Brian came equipped with everything she needed to reach nirvana.

This god of a man sat up on his knees. "Now, *that* was what I wanted to hear." He looked so pleased with himself, his hair a mess, his eyes shining with pride. "Let me get a condom on and then you can tell me where you want me next. On top, with your tits in my face sounds pretty damn good to me."

She gave him a sideways look. "You've been carrying around condoms all this time?" She couldn't help but wonder about their expiration date.

A smile stretched wide across his face. With his index finger, he scratched his temple, his eyes sheepish. "Well, not exactly. I was hoping my apology would win me a few favors." His expression flattened as he raised a palm of caution. "Is that cool? I didn't mean to be presumptuous. Or expect anything in return." His cheeks heated up like a burner on a hot stove. "You don't owe me anything."

Watching him unravel like a ball of yarn, Sophie giggled. "It's more than okay. And of course I know that." She beckoned him as she rolled onto her stomach. "Now get over here. I like the sound of your next plan."

* * *

Covered in a sheen of sweat, Sophie fell back onto her pillow. "That was intense. I've never orgasmed that hard or that often."

All she could think about was how bad in bed the men she'd slept with were before now. With Chad, she'd barely eeked out an orgasm, and even then, it wasn't often. The toys were for *his* benefit, not hers.

Battering-ram Chad sucked in bed.

Propped up on his elbow, Brian leaned over her. "Glad to be of service, my lady." As he said those words, he saluted her in a playful sort of way.

Sophie ran a hand over his strong shoulder and down his rugged arm. "Oh, you were of service, all right. What I want to know is where you small-town men learn all of *those* moves?"

No matter what position they tried, and they tried a few— her on top, side to side, her straddling him on the chair in the corner, Brian focused on her needs. His fingers found regions of her female body that had never been more excited to meet a man. One thing was clear, this guy knew his way around a woman's anatomy.

"I'll never tell." Releasing a short snicker, Brian hopped out of bed and strode through the open alcove of her vanity and into her bathroom, his butt cheeks plump and muscular, providing her with a perfect view. "Be right back, beautiful."

As water ran into her bathroom sink, Sophie propped her pillows up and watched Brian through the mirror in front of him. He finger brushed his teeth, then set to washing a fresh layer of *her* off his facial hair. And there was a lot of *her* on it. When he returned to her bed, he snuggled up next to her, a minty scent wafting off his lips mixed in with a hint of lemongrass drying on his beard from her hand soap. It was a nice combination.

"Well, I would say that that was a successful venture, wouldn't you?" He brought his woolly chin up next to hers.

"Oh, yeah." She bent her arm back, embracing his head from behind her. "What time is it, anyway?"

Brian rolled onto his back. "Clock over here says three-thirty. I guess we lost track of time."

Sophie yawned. "Cuddle up next to me, you big bear. I need a nap."

"I can't stay much longer, but I'll wait until you fall asleep." With his mouth next to her ear, he nestled into her, wrapping her blanket over them both. "I know this is a touchy subject, but I think you should try talking to your parents about Chad. Have you hired a lawyer yet?"

Sophie was glad he couldn't see her face when she said, "Not yet." She swallowed, a lump of remorse forming in her throat. "I plan to, though. My parents aren't easy. You have no idea." They were the main reason she hadn't filed yet.

Brian pulled her closer. "Do you have any relatives that you're close to?"

"There is someone. Well, two someones, actually. He's not a relative, but I'm close to an elderly man named Charlie and his wife Ginny. Charlie used to manage the grounds at my parents' estate. He and I were always close. He's known me my whole life." Memories of Charlie mowing the lawn while Sophie sat nearby reading a book or doing her homework sprang to life in her mind. When she'd scraped her knees running too fast, he tended to her wounds. When her mother scolded her repeatedly, he wiped her tears. He taught her to drive and even attended both of her graduations with Ginny by his side, something her mother objected to, but her father allowed.

"He's the one who lives in Charlottesville, right?" Brian's breath tickled her ear.

"Yup."

"Good. Then go see him." Brian sat up as if trying to make an impact. "You have my full support, Soph, but it would also be nice if you spoke to someone who knows your family. See what he thinks. And I'd get working on that lawyer. I know of a few good lawyers who could take on your case."

She rolled over to face him. "First of all, *Soph?*" Is that your nickname for me? She grinned from ear to ear at the thought. No one had called her Soph before. The Quinns were too formal for nicknames. And Chad just didn't give enough of a shit. *Dearest?* Who called his wife by such a formal nickname?

Using his fingers, Brian gently laced a few long strands of her hair behind her ear. "Is that okay?"

She sighed. "Of course it's okay. But only you get to call me that. Charlie calls me Poppy because of my obsession with bubblegum when I was little."

Raising the blanket as he bent one knee, Brian rested his forearm on his leg and chuckled. "Oh, yeah? Poppy, huh? Did your parents have a nickname for you?"

Sophie made a raspberry with her lips. "Yeah, pain in the ass." She was kidding, of course, but not really. "Hey, how come we never talk about you?" She feigned indignation as she sat up. "Considering what we just did together, could I at least get a last name?" She placed a hand on her hip. It was strange not knowing these things already.

"Hughes," Brian said as he cleared his throat in an almost uncomfortable way.

He'd acted similarly when she'd asked him for his cell phone number. But he didn't know her then. What was his deal now? Sophie chose to let it go.

"Okay, now we're getting somewhere. And how do you know a few good lawyers who can take on my case? Have you worked on their houses or something?" She stared with intent, trying to figure this man out.

Brian fell back onto his pillow, his arm draped over his forehead. "Yeah, I've worked for a few people who may be able to help you. And I'm a simple guy. Not much to tell." His voice dipped as he spoke, and Sophie wondered if something bad had happened to him.

She hoped not.

"Well, tell me one thing, then. I want to know one new thing about a man who can make me orgasm three times in one night."

Keeping his arm draped, Brian seemed to think about that. "My mother died when I was six. It was during a freak storm. A tree fell on her car and crushed her. It was a miracle that I wasn't with her. I don't remember much about her, just flashes here and there. My dad raised me. He and I have remained tight."

Sophie sank down next to him, her hand caressing his bare chest, which she was surprised to discover wasn't as hairy as she would have expected. "I'm so sorry. That must've been rough. I can't imagine going through something like that. You poor thing." She rested her chin on his rib cage and stared up, her heart feeling his sorrow. "I'm glad you still have your dad."

Brian lifted his arm away from his forehead, touching her cheek. "My dad's great. He'd do anything for me. And vice versa."

"That's nice, Brian. I wish my dad ..." Sophie shook her head, trying to reset herself. This wasn't about her. "Thank you for sharing that with me. I hope I get to meet him someday. And Julian, too. I know he's a good friend of yours." She sat up this time, resting back on her ankles. "I meant to tell you that on the last segment of 'Where in the world is Julian Sommers?' they interviewed Rebecca's parents."

Brian inched his body up against her headboard, his brow furrowed. "Sorry excuse for parents, if you ask me." He pointed, his cheeks firing up. "They were the reason Rebecca was so fucked up. Don't get me wrong. I'm sorry for their loss. To lose a kid must have been the worst. But to make money from it?" He shook his head in disgust, his lips tightening into a thin line.

"Yeah, that was obvious in the interview. Poor Julian. It sounded like they tried to take advantage of him financially, and even after he helped them, they still acted like it was Julian's fault. Fucking losers."

When he didn't respond, Sophie leaned into Brian, cupping his jaw with her palm. His eyes grew distant, his face contorted with anger. "Julian still believes it was *his* fault. I can't seem to convince him otherwise."

Sophie remembered the anger in Julian's tone through the intercom. "It's not his fault, though. There's nothing he could have done."

"That's what I've said to him, over and over again."

"How does Julian respond to that?"

"He says, 'He could have helped her.'"

"Next time you talk to him, ask him this. If you knew that Rebecca was capable of murder or suicide, would you have done anything differently?" She paused. "My guess is yes. And there lies the problem. He didn't know. We can't see our future, and we certainly can't predict what another person is thinking. I saw Rebecca's parents. And I did a little research on Rebecca. She'd been arrested for prostitution more than once, and she was homeless. If there is blame to be cast, it's on her parents. Not Julian."

Brian tipped his head from side to side as he considered this. "He said he did try to help her once, but she disappeared. The next time he saw her was in that hotel room."

Sophie gave his arm a light slap. "See. He *did* try to help. She wasn't willing to accept his help. If anyone was victimized, it was Julian. *Not* Rebecca. She was a ticking time bomb, waiting to go off."

Brian firmed his brow. "Don't forget, an innocent woman was murdered."

"That doesn't change the reality of the situation, Brian. It just makes it more unfortunate." She nudged his shoulder. "Keep talking sense to him. Eventually, you'll get through."

Brian seemed to ponder this as a quiet moment tiptoed between them, one that Sophie was hoping to turn around. This had been too special an evening to end it on a sad note.

"Hey. I didn't mean to bring that up. I know he's your friend, *Bri*."

The ghost of a smile washed over Brian's somber expression. "Bri? Is that payback for Soph?"

She wiggled her shoulders a tad. "Well, that can be our nicknames for each other. No one gets to call us that but us." She made a dismissive gesture with her hand. "Unless, of course, your father or close friends already do call you Bri."

Brian maneuvered himself forward until he was right in front of her face. He kissed her plump lips. "Nope. No one calls me Bri. It's all yours."

As they slid back under the sheets, covered up, and nestled into each other, Sophie felt such a feeling of contentment. It was both bizarre and scary for her. In fact, she wasn't sure she had ever felt it before. Oh sure, there were moments when her family actually came together, like one Christmas when her dad dressed up as Santa and surprised them all, or when he sprang for a tropical vacation where they scuba dived, sailed, and lounged by the pool. And even the time he took them all to dinner after she had graduated from college. *"To Sophie, my pride and joy. We are so proud of you."* It was a toast for the ages. The problem was that those moments were fleeting. The positive vibe snuffed out as soon as regular life settled in, the chill returning to their home and their hearts. What she felt with Brian was different. She hoped—no, she prayed—it was real, and did she even dare to say, permanent? She could get used to having him in her life.

She'd go see Charlie, and she'd tell him what had happened. He'd want to know, and he'd also know how best to handle her parents. It was a good idea.

She clicked off her lamp and rested her head on her pillow, her man spooning her, his warmth settling into her bones.

Keeping her voice extremely low, she whispered the words, "I love you, Bri." She knew he wouldn't be able to hear her, but she had to say it anyway.

"Love you, too, Soph."

# Chapter Eight

That Saturday, she awoke to bright sunshine streaming through her windows, the sound of a lawn mower purring across her property.

*Charlie!*

Sophie sprang out of bed, threw on some comfy clothes, and ran out to greet him. Not only had she given him a key to her cottage, but she'd also made sure he had one for the garage where her riding mower sat ready and waiting to groom her lawn.

"Hey, there." She waved her arms over her head until Charlie took notice and steered in her direction. As the mower rumbled to a stop, Charlie beamed a smile.

"Beautiful mornin'. Thought I'd get an early start." Charlie removed his straw hat that looked like it belonged in the outback and wiped his forearm across his brow. "I hope I didn't wake you, Poppy."

Sophie met him at the mower, where she leaned in for a hug, her nose confronted with scents of fresh grass and exhaust. "Nope. I was awake." She wasn't. "Got time for breakfast afterward? I could scramble us up some eggs? Brew some coffee?"

Charlie placed his hat back on his head and glanced at his watch, a retirement gift from Sophie's father.

Johnathan Quinn had a soft spot for Charlie, and it glistened on his wrist, the Rolex not quite representing the old man's humble demeanor. Most men wouldn't be wearing the Oystersteel and yellow-gold watch that cost close to twenty-thousand dollars (Sophie helped her father pick it out) while doing manual labor, but that was so Charlie, who probably had no concept of its monetary value.

"Well, Ginny's sister is in town, and we were planning on taking her to Monticello. She's in from Pittsburgh, and Ginny has wanted to show her around some sites now that we live nearby."

"Oh, okay. No problem." Sophie's shoulders slumped, her voice dipping low. Maybe she could visit him this week, then. She turned to leave.

"Wait. I guess I'm almost done here. Suppose I could have a few eggs and a cup of Joe." He smiled, his pale-blue eyes getting paler with age.

Her spirits lifted. "Are you sure?"

He pushed the clutch for the mower, his hand on the ignition key. "You go make us some breakfast, Poppy, and I'll be right along." *Varoom.* The mower growled to life, its wheels eager to finish the job.

"Somethin' on your mind, Poppy?" Charlie had just taken his last bite of eggs, his coffee nearly empty. He stared across the kitchen table at Sophie, his eyes doing their best to evaluate the situation.

Sophie knew her time with him was coming to an end but, somehow, couldn't seem to come out with it. *Chad abused me sexually. He tried to choke me to death as he screwed me raw.* Nope. That wouldn't work. If she said that, Charlie would hyperventilate all over her kitchen, not a good prequel for their visit to Monticello.

Charlie sat back in his seat, his hands resting on the table. He exhaled. "I know what's weighing on you, Poppy."

Sophie's chin sprang up, her eyebrows lifting in surprise. "You do?"

Charlie nodded once. "You and Chad been havin' some problems, I take it?"

Now, it was Sophie's turn to nod.

"Well, how bad is it? Can you reconcile? Or is it too far gone?"

Sophie studied her answer. "Do you like Chad, Charlie?"

He adjusted the waist of his pants, his jaw working on something. "Don't matter much what I think." He met her gaze. "The question is, Poppy, do you like him?"

Man, he was good at batting a question right back at her. Always had been. Charlie liked to help people find their own solutions in life. Realizing their time was short, she finally owned up to her answer. "No, I don't like him. He's not who everyone thinks he is."

"Oh?" Charlie watched her with pinpoint precision. The same precision that had kept their family's lawns manicured to perfection for years.

Sophie placed the palms of her hands on the table's surface, the coolness of the wood refreshing against her skin. "He's gotten abusive with me." *That's safe, right?* She didn't say sexually.

"Do your parents know about this?" His expression hardened, his eyes trying to read her.

Sophie shook her head in exasperation. "You know my mom. She loves Chad. And my dad's never around. I don't know if either of them would even support me." Her hair up in a ponytail, she started twirling the loose ends at the back of her neck. "I want to divorce him, Charlie. I can't live with him anymore. It's just not possible."

Charlie rubbed his jaw contemplatively. "And counseling is out of the question?"

"Not after what he did to—" She bit her lower lip to stop herself from finishing her sentence.

Charlie's brow rose with concern. "What did he do to you, Poppy?" He reached his wrinkled hand out to cover one of hers. "You can tell me. It's okay. I've always been here for you, and I always will be."

That did it. The waterworks. Her eyes flooded with tears. She pushed her chair back and wept into her hands. Apparently, crying was her thing now.

Within seconds, Charlie was at her side, consoling her, his arm around her back. "There, there. It's gonna be okay, Poppy. You don't have to tell me. I'm sorry I pushed you." He left her side, but only to grab a box of tissues from a side table in the living room, returning a moment later with the box in his hand.

"I'm sorry. I didn't mean to—"

"You've nothing to be sorry about." He handed her some tissues, which she used to sop up her tears.

Charlie's tone changed. "I haven't seen you cry since you were a sprout." He patted her head. "And it just breaks my heart to see you this way. Ginny and I will be here for you for whatever lies ahead." He pulled a chair closer so he could sit at her level. His knees were not capable of kneeling at this stage of his life, and he knew better than to push it.

"I know my mom won't support me." Sophie sniffled and whined, the tissue tight in her palm.

Charlie spoke with a soft voice, one meant to console. "Well, your mother has aways had a hard way about her, no doubt. I have to admit, she never warmed up to me, nor I to her. But your dad loves you, Poppy, more than you know."

Strange how he didn't defend her mother.

"Talk to your dad. Catch him when he's alone. He'll listen. I know he'll listen. Give him a chance to help his daughter." He grabbed hold of her hand and squeezed. "I know we're old, but we will always be here for you as long as we're still kickin'." He gazed at his watch. "Oh. I better get goin'. Ginny will have my hide if I'm late." He slid his chair back, his hand finding her head one last time. "I never liked Chad. You can always tell a lot about a man by the way he treats the help. That one has always reminded me of a snake, the kind that bites ya when ya ain't lookin'."

Laughter bubbled up through Sophie's tears. "You can say that again." She stood and escorted Charlie to the door. He'd always been her constant, someone she could rely on to be there for her. He'd lost *his* daughter, and she'd often wondered if maybe being there for Sophie had helped him in some way. Or maybe Sophie just chose to think that it had. Justine had been gone for over two decades, yet Sophie knew so little about her. "You don't talk about your daughter much. Is that because it's too painful?"

A shadow drifted over Charlie's eyes, one filled with loss and heartache. "I guess you're right, Poppy. But it's not because I don't think the world of her. Justine was the apple of my eye. And her mother's. Never liked to sit still. Always runnin' in one direction or another, searching for a good cause." He sighed, his eyes unfocused. "She had a heart of gold."

"I remember seeing pictures of her when she was a baby. Remember those times when I came to your place?"

Visits to Charlie and Ginny's ranch-style house were rare,

mainly because Cecilia disapproved of her daughter fraternizing with the help. But every now and then, Charlie would find an excuse to take Sophie to the nursery with him to help pick out flowers or bushes for the estate. In those isolated instances, they'd make a quick stop by to see Ginny, who always had a cookie or two prepared for Sophie. They'd sit on their front porch and talk about fun shows they were watching, boys, and annoying teachers (not always in that order). Inside, baby pictures of their precious daughter adorned their mantel and a few shelves in their modest-sized living room, smiling away with glee. At times, Sophie wished *she* was their daughter, but she never told anyone for fear of retribution.

"I remember," Charlie said, his face drawn, his eyes reflective of another time.

They'd lost a great deal, Sophie could tell. But if she'd learned anything about life lately, it was to embrace the special gifts, not shy away from them. Being with Brian had taught her that. "Maybe someday you can tell me more about Justine. Coming from you and Ginny, she must've been quite a beauty. And even though her heart wasn't strong enough to sustain a long life, I know that you and Ginny filled her heart with all of the love you had while she was here." Raising up on her tiptoes, Sophie kissed Charlie on the cheek.

She opened the front door. "Give my best to Ginny, and have fun at Monticello." She watched him walk down the path toward his truck. "I'll come by sometime soon for a visit."

Charlie stopped and turned to face her. "Ginny would like that. And good luck with your dad. Please let me know how it goes."

As Sophie awaited the arrival of her father at a popular downtown restaurant in the historic section of Richmond, she found herself a bundle of nerves. On Sunday he kept his office closed, although Johnathan Quinn never really stopped working. She'd called him the night before. "Hey, Dad. I need to talk with you about something important. Could you meet me for lunch or brunch? Just the two of us?" she'd asked.

"Uh," he said, not sounding glad at all to hear from her. "I'm swamped with work, Sophie. Chad and I are trying to land a new client. A big one. This partnership is going to take this company right into the—"

"You don't need to pitch to me, Dad. It's fine. I get it." Disappointment laced her words.

She pulled her cell phone away from her ear just as the words "Wait, wait, don't hang up" begged for another chance.

"Yeah?"

"Sure. I can meet you. I don't have time to drive out there. Can you come to the house? I'd like to find out more about what you're doing in that part of the state anyway."

No way was she meeting him at home, and for one very good reason. Cecilia. "As I said, I'd like it to be just the two of us. How about lunch downtown?"

So there she was, waiting at one of the finest restaurants in Richmond, the seats cushioned, the table cloth stark white, and the menu expensive. She sipped on a mimosa, hoping it would bring her courage, the orange juice tangy on her taste buds, the champagne doing its best to keep her from bolting. Her dad loved Chad. He'd made him his VP. He was his son-in-law. How in the world could she convince him that he was bad news for his daughter?

"You've got this, Soph," Brian had told her when she'd left him in her bed that morning.

He'd come by for an early morning roll in the sheets, and

she was so glad he had. The smell of his earthly scent on her skin, the feel of him between her legs, still very real. He hadn't slept an entire night with her, but she was optimistic it would happen soon.

"Charlie wouldn't tell you to do this unless he thought it would be okay."

How Brian seemed to know Charlie better than her family did was beyond her. But she'd painted a picture of Charlie for Brian, one colored with love and trust.

Her cell phone chimed on the table. It was a text from her dad: *Here.*

She took a few deep, cleansing breaths. Okay, you can do this. *He's your father, not your parole officer.*

Her father came shuffling through the door, his suit pressed, his hair slicked back, and his aura ever so distinguished. And riding on his coattails came Chad.

"What the hell?" she said out loud as the duo approached, the acids in her stomach boiling like water on a hot stove. Her pits started to sweat. Her hands knotted in her lap.

"What a nice surprise." Chad leaned in, landing a poisonous kiss on her cheek, one that she wanted to wipe away immediately. His gaze scanned over her flowing tangerine shirt dress with a yellow belt. "When your father told me he was having lunch with you here today, I wasn't going to miss a chance to see my beautiful wife." Clothed in expensive *and* matching golf attire and smelling like he'd dumped half a bottle of cologne over his head, Chad stood back with his hands on his hips feigning outrage. "Although I have to admit, I'm a little insulted you didn't call your husband first."

Johnathan sat in the chair across from Sophie, his eyes filled with skepticism. All directed at his daughter, no doubt.

Chad took the seat adjacent from her.

Wearing a crisp white shirt, black tie, and black pants, a

waitress appeared with their menus, her blonde hair pulled tight into a bun. "Can I start you gentlemen off with a mimosa as well?"

Johnathan's phone chimed. He shook his head at the waitress and mouthed, *coffee*, as he took the call, got up from the table, and walked outside.

"And for you, sir?" The waitress waited for Chad to answer.

"Sure, I'll take a mimosa and a coffee as well."

"Very good, sir." She fanned a hand out toward the restaurant's guest of honor: the buffet. "And we have a fabulous buffet today with a carving station and dessert bar."

Scents of garlic, roasted beef, and sugary confections had Sophie's mouth watering for at least ten minutes now, her stomach growling with anticipation. But since Chad had arrived, her appetite had taken a nosedive.

"Plates are over there for you." She smiled and clapped her hands together. "Help yourself whenever you're ready, and I will get those beverages for you right away. Miss, would you like another?"

"Oh, yeah," Sophie grumbled as the waitress departed in search of their drinks.

Chad watched her go, his gaze glued to her ass. Then he turned to his wife. "So, trying to meet with Daddy without me, huh?" Chad's sickly-sweet tone had morphed into the real Chad. The asshalf had resurfaced.

Sophie guzzled the rest of her drink, then smacked her lips. "So what if I am? I don't need your permission to have brunch with *my* father." She smiled at him in a venomous sort of way, the kind that said *fuck you.*

Chad took hold of her hand, which sat resting on the table. And then he squeezed. "What's going on, dearest? You wouldn't be thinking of telling your father lies about me, would you?"

Sophie gritted her teeth. "Lies? Or the truth?"

He squeezed harder.

"Here we are." The waitress placed two mimosas on the table. She then flipped over two coffee mugs resting on saucers (Sophie had already passed on the coffee) and filled them with the steaming hot liquid. She'd already delivered a small sterling-silver creamer and tray of sweeteners.

Chad released Sophie's hand, which she slid immediately under the table to stretch out the pain. She didn't want Chad to see how much he had hurt her.

When had he become so abusive? Had he always been this way, and she'd never noticed? Sophie was really starting to question herself.

When they were alone again, Chad took a generous sip of his drink and leaned closer to Sophie. "Look. I know you're not happy with me. And I can't say that I'm thrilled with you, either. But we have an arrangement."

Sophie's cheeks flared, her stomach doing its best to prevent an eruption. "I never agreed to anything. I want a divorce, Chad." *Shit, why did you just play your trump card?*

In the distance, Johnathan finished up his call and headed in their direction.

Chad softened his tone. "I didn't realize things had gotten that far. Let's not be hasty."

"I'm not being hasty. I'm being serious. I want a divorce."

Glancing at Johnathan's approach, he whisper-shouted, "Well, you can't have one! You need to give me some time to figure things out."

*Figure what out? How to murder me in my sleep?*

"Sorry about the interruption. Shall we?" Johnathan

gestured toward the impressive buffet emitting flurries of tantalizing scents throughout the restaurant.

"No, thanks." Sophie stood. "I'm not hungry. And, Dad, I asked to meet with you alone, but I can see that you are never alone." She glanced down at Chad, who scowled at her while trying to mask his annoyance. "Chad and I have been separated for over six months, Father. We've grown apart." She watched Chad's face darken to the color of a tomato. "I am going to hire a lawyer." She thought about her next words very carefully. Did she want to make Chad her enemy? Or did she want a clean break and a new life of her own? Maybe one with Brian? "It's nobody's fault. We've been together since high school, and like I said, we've grown apart."

Her father's face fell. "Is that why you moved away?" He glared at Chad, then returned his gaze to his daughter, standing before him.

As if Sophie was a ticking time bomb, Chad continued to watch her with trepidation, waiting for the shrapnel of her words to pierce his egotistical facade.

"I asked Chad not to tell you that, Father. I wanted to see if we could work things out. We can't. I want to stay in my cottage and work remotely. I need to speak with my boss about that. I'm starting a new life out there, and I love it." She smiled at the two stunned faces, making her gulp inwardly. Then she lifted the strap of her purse off the back of her chair and cleared her throat. "I trust you will enjoy your brunch. Good day, gentlemen." Feeling more like a board member than a relative, she turned on her heel and walked out.

"Don't forget to stop and see your mother on your way out of town. She knows you're here and isn't happy that you didn't tell her you were coming."

*Argh.* That stopped Sophie in her tracks. She was fuming. "Fine. And thanks for the father-daughter time. Let's do this again sometime, shall we?" She didn't know where that last statement came from. She was angry. And she was right. Her father wouldn't support her. Now, she had to face her mother's wrath. If Sophie were a betting woman, she'd guess Cecilia would already know the news before Sophie arrived.

* * *

Feeling as if she'd just swallowed a grenade, her insides rattled and uneasy, Sophie pushed her hybrid's accelerator, heading toward her parents' estate. Instead of taking the interstate, she chose a side road, only to get stuck in construction. *Perfect! What now?* She just wanted to get this over with.

When she finally arrived, Cecilia was waiting out front for her daughter, her chin high and her arms crossed over her fake chest.

She was right. Her father had informed Cecilia of Sophie's desire to divorce Chad, long before she had pulled into the circular driveway.

As Sophie approached, her mother stared her down.

"I can't believe you want to throw everything you and Chad have built together down the drain." Her arms went from crossed to one hand braced over each hip. "Have you lost your mind? Are you on drugs? Is that it? Do I need to put you in rehab?"

*No, Hello, Sophie, nice to see you. Do you want to talk about it?* That only happened on sitcoms in Sophie's world.

"No, I'm not on drugs, Mother. And Chad is not who you think he is."

Cecilia was so angry her head shook, like a tea kettle ready to blow steam in every direction. "What are you talking about? Chad is the best thing that's ever happened to you. He loves you." She stormed into the house, Sophie on her designer heels.

"No, he doesn't love me, Mother. And he is not the best thing that has ever happened to me. Not even close. He's abusive and cruel. And the only reason he kisses your's and dad's asses on a regular basis is because he wants what you have: money and power. He's threatened me more than once if I did anything to mess up his plans."

If Cecilia were a radio, she had tuned her daughter out, no longer receiving anything Sophie had to say. "There is nothing wrong with making plans. You've been together for eight years, and you haven't even given him a child. Have you ever thought that maybe he wanted a family? If he's acting out, that's probably why."

*A child?* Sophie's head hurt, trying to make sense of her mother's logic. She flailed a hand in the air as they both entered the formal living room, her mother making a stand near their baby grand with its own alcove, curved windows framing it. "What are you talking about, Mother? We were in high school and college for six of those years. And trust me, he doesn't want—"

"But I do, dearest." Blinking over a full set of puppy dog eyes, Chad appeared, the corners of his mouth crimping downward.

Two seconds later, her father joined their family meeting. It was an ambush.

"What is this? Are you all ganging up on me now?"

Chad approached, his palms raised in full surrender mode. "No, not at all. I'm so sorry that you aren't happy. And I'm sorry if I made you feel that my job with your dad's company was more important than you are. I love you, Sophie. Always have." He reached out to her with his bluish-gray eyes, his whole demeanor meant to fool the fools around her.

She wasn't buying it. "Don't. I mean it, Chad." Her frayed nerves had her gritting her teeth.

Shaking her head, Cecilia flung her manicured hand in the air. "Don't what? Love you? Are you determined to ruin your life just to make a point?"

"That's okay, Cecilia. She's right to be angry with me. I've been neglecting my wife. I deserve this." By now, Chad had moved into position—right in front of Sophie's face. He reached down and took her hand, which she yanked away.

Sophie searched for her father. He stood near the wide opening to the foyer, watching, observing, but not saying a word. That was what this was all about: Chad performing for them. And if he were a good enough actor, they'd believe everything he said.

Sophie's muscles were as tight as a piano string, ready to unravel at any moment. The mimosas in her stomach sloshed around like the bottom of a leaky boat. She was used to feeling alone. But after experiencing life on her own these past several months, her outlook had started to change. And after meeting Brian, she now knew things didn't have to be that way. No one was going to take that hope away from her. Not her parents and not Chad.

"All I ask is that you give me a little more time to try to convince you otherwise. If you want to get away, I can book us a ticket tonight anywhere you want to go. You are all that matters to me, and I won't lose you without a fight." With gentle fingers, he brushed a few strands of her hair over her shoulder. "You are, and will always be, the love of my life."

If Sophie could have gagged without looking like a total bitch, she would have. Stuck her finger right down her throat and let it rip. She was a lot of things, but stupid wasn't one of them. If she came off too cold and heartless, that was how they would see her. By they, she meant her parents. She didn't give a shit what Chad thought.

*Think.*

"I can't go away with you right now. I'm working on some cases that need my attention at work." It was only half true. She was busy, but not *so* busy she couldn't have one of her colleagues help her out.

"Isn't your marriage more important than your volunteering?"

Sophie snapped her head in her mother's direction. "I'm not volunteering, Mother, I'm getting paid."

Cecilia made a *pfft* through her bright-colored lips.

"Let's all just take a minute. Come. Let's sit." Chad gestured toward the elongated sofa and chairs designed to impress but not comfort.

The group made their way over, Sophie's father choosing the arm chair next to where Sophie sat. Was that meant in support of her? Sophie didn't have a clue. The man still hadn't uttered a word since he'd arrived.

Cecilia and Chad took to the sofa as one united front across from father and daughter, a large glass coffee table separating the poles.

Chad scooted to the edge of the sofa cushion, his hands clasped between his thighs. "I don't think this separation has been good for us."

Sophie opened her mouth to object, but Chad raised a palm. "Hear me out. You've been gone for months. And in the meantime, we haven't gone to any counseling or done anything together to see if we can work things through. It would be better for our marriage if you moved home so that we can work on *us*."

All eyes rested on Sophie. Moving home was not an option. She couldn't go back to that house. She couldn't sleep next to that monster. "I like where I am. I'm happy there." The words barely escaped her lips, her confidence shredding like confetti.

Cecilia crossed her legs, her spine as straight as a yardstick.

"You have a beautiful home here. And a husband who wants to be with you." She fiddled with her diamond bracelet. "That is more than most people have. You have been brought up with privilege, Sophie. We have given you everything."

"Except your love and support." Sophie sounded so weak, so defeated. And so young. Like a ten-year-old.

Her father turned to her. "What did you say?"

Sophie stared down at her lap. "Nothing. It doesn't matter." *Don't you dare cry.*

Chad leaned even closer to the coffee table. Any farther and he'd hit the floor. "Sophie, I love you. You're my wife. Before we throw everything we have down the drain, don't you think it's worth finding out if we can fix things? Don't you think our marriage deserves that?" He tilted his head, his eyes continuing to implore her.

Did he care about their marriage when he nearly choked her to death while fucking the shit out of her? *"Don't worry. I'm not going to hurt you."* He'd lied. Did he care about their marriage when he ignored who she was and what she wanted to do with her life? Every time she tried to reach out to him over the years, he'd wave her off. *"I've got a phone call to make." "I don't have time for this right now."* Once again, it wasn't until Sophie had met Brian that she realized how badly Chad had been treating her. And then Chad's words from just the other day echoed in her head. *"Don't fuck with me, Sophie. I've worked too hard to get where I am, and I won't let you ruin this for me."*

Unable to provide a verbal answer, Sophie stood, her limbs heavy, her heart breaking apart. What was left of it anyway. "I can't move home right now. I just can't." There was that ten-year-old tone again. *Damn it.* She wanted to be strong.

Chad also stood. "Why not? What's out there that you can't leave behind for your marriage?"

The location had nothing to do with it. It was all about getting away from *him*.

She couldn't think. She couldn't find the right words to push back against his reasoning, as flawed as it was. All that was left was her honesty. "I already told you. I'm happy out there. You don't make me happy, Chad. You never have. And up until today, you've never even tried. We are too different. I don't want the same things you do. I'm sorry. I just don't. I can't do this anymore." She took a step away from the firing line. "I'm sorry. Whatever you want in the divorce, you can have. I won't contest it. Please, just give me my freedom."

"That's just about enough of your drivel!" Cecilia flew to her feet. "How dare you speak to your husband that way. I don't know who you think you are. You were lucky he chose someone like you."

"Cecilia, that's enough." Finally, her father rose to his feet and joined the conversation.

Sophie mashed her teeth together. Pretty soon, she'd have nothing but nubs. "Someone like me, Mother? What does *that* mean? You've never supported any of my decisions." She raised a defiant finger. "Correction. You've only supported one: me marrying Chad. I'm tired of you looking down your nose at me. What did I ever do to make you hate me so much?" She could understand why Cecilia had struggled with Sophie's father. He'd checked out years ago. But there were times when Sophie had tried to console her mother. She hated the names her father had called her mother, *ice queen* being one of them.

When her parents had argued once and her father had stormed out of the house, proclaiming Cecilia was unloveable, Sophie even went so far as to try to hug her mother, hoping to let her know she wasn't alone. "It's okay, Mommy. I'm here."

The embrace lasted for about five seconds before her mother flung her arms out, and eight-year-old Sophie fell backward onto the Italian marble kitchen floor, hitting her head in the process. Her mother never even apologized. She just stood and walked out of the room, her posture stiff as a soldier.

Instead of answering her now, Cecilia huffed, her fingers touching up the edges of her bobbed hairdo. "That's preposterous. As usual, you're not making any sense."

Sophie spread her hands out. "Don't you want me to be happy? Do you even care?"

A layer of storm clouds rose over Cecilia's head, her eyes boring holes in Sophie's defense system. "Happy?" Slowly, she swung one arm out, the way a game show host would do. "You have everything anyone could ever need. But it's never enough for you." She gestured toward Chad, standing nearby. "You have a loving husband who wants to be with you. You've always had privilege, but you snub your nose at it. I'm sick and tired of you taking everything we've given you for granted." Her eyes burned with newfound fury. "You're a spoiled brat, and you don't deserve any of this."

A subtle smirk played on Chad's lips. Although he tried to hide it, he was clearly enjoying the show.

Not her father, though, whose shoulders were rising by the second. "Knock it off, Cecilia. You're not helping matters."

Another huff sounded like an alarm from her mother's pursed lips. "And *you*. You always let her get away with everything. The girl needed discipline." She waved an angry hand in Johnathan's direction. "It if were up to you, she'd be galavanting around with hoodlums, probably pregnant and living in squalor by now." She used one fist to pound her other palm. "She needed discipline ... and structure. She needed *me* to turn her into a lady. Lord knows she wasn't getting it anywhere else. You think I enjoyed raising a girl who prefers street rats to decent people?" She chuckled with no humor involved.

"Maybe that's what she deserves." If her chin had risen any higher, she'd be hitting the ceiling.

Sophie couldn't believe her ears. Who were the street rats? She'd been with Chad forever, it seemed, and she certainly wasn't talking about him.

"Knock it off! I'm warning you, Cecilia."

She gritted her teeth at her husband. "I won't knock anything off. This has gone on for far too long. You should be grateful for everything I've done for her. You were never around. It was always up to me. You think it's normal for a young woman to hang out with our gardener? You think that's healthy? That crazy old man was probably a pervert for all you knew."

*Charlie?* How could she say that? He was a saint. Whatever loss in gumption Sophie was feeling, Cecilia's insults had revitalized her. She stomped over to her mother and pointed at her plastic face. "Don't you dare speak ill of Charlie. He has always been there for me."

"Jesus Christ, Cecilia. This isn't the time. I need you to stop talking right now." Johnathan had fists dangling from his sides, a wrinkle the size of a crater forged across his forehead.

In Sophie's periphery, Chad's eyes shined with amusement, his hand half-covering his smirk. He only did that because her father wasn't watching. *What an ass.*

Cecilia's face twisted with ire. "I will not be silenced. That's why she acts the way she does. She's always sought out the dregs of society. I got her away from those lowlifes in high school. And if it were up to me, I would've had that old coot thrown off our property ... or put in jail. You want her to act like a lady of society? I *had* to be tough. But what good did I do?" She blew out her lips.

Before Sophie knew what was happening, her hand flew up and smacked her mother across the face. "How dare you say that about Charlie. He's meant more to me than you ever will. I hate you!" She glared at her father. "Charlie told me to come talk to you. He said you'd listen. He was giving you assholes way too much credit."

Instead of acting stunned or reacting in any way from the physical strike, a catlike grin took over Cecilia's lips. "See, Johnathan. Street rat." She said the words with perfect poise.

That was all Sophie could take. She turned and ran as fast as her feet would carry her—out of that godforsaken house and away from her circus of a family.

# Chapter Nine

"I'm sorry, Soph, that sounds rough," Brian said through the car speakers as Sophie drove west and away from Richmond.

She released a heavy sigh, her cheeks drying from tears. The closer she came to home—her home—the better she felt. "It was. Do you believe my mother called me a street rat? And Charlie one, too? I always knew she never liked my relationship with him, but, Brian, he's a harmless old man. And Ginny is a sweetheart."

"If it's any consolation, when I first got my learner's permit, my dad called me worse. Of course I had driven his truck through our closed garage door, so I guess I can't blame the man." He chuckled before his tone grew more serious. "Sorry. Not the same thing. Do you think she's jealous? You said you two aren't exactly close. And you and Charlie are."

Sophie thought about that as she pulled the visor down to shield her eyes from the springtime sun, dried pollen coating the edges of her windshield, the Blue Ridge Mountains growing greener by the day. "No, I think she's a snob who can't stand anyone in her family having a relationship with someone she feels is beneath her." It was a terrible way for anyone to think about their mother, but what other conclusion could Sophie draw? She couldn't imagine what Cecilia would think of Brian. That was a battle she'd have to fight another day. Or another decade, considering how bad things were going.

"I sort of slapped her across the face for it."

"You did what?" Brian's voice boomed through the car's speakers. "Man, you Quinn women really go at it."

"It's never happened before. Well, she's slapped me a few times, but I've never slapped her back." Sophie felt ashamed for doing it at all. Not a proud moment for her. "She's just such a bitch. And she doesn't seem to like my dad much, either, but he's been cheating on her for years." *Did I just say that?* How had Brian become her confessional? She seemed so comfortable telling him just about anything these days.

"Wow. Your dad's been cheating on your mom? Does she know?"

An ounce of sympathy squeezed from Sophie's heart. "I'm sure she does. I don't like that about my dad." Sophie grew quiet. "My mom is a hard woman to love, but I do love her." She felt she needed to say that.

"Of course you do. I get it. It's okay to be pissed off at her, though."

"I've only met *her* mother, Grandma DuBois, a few times, and she's even colder, trust me. I don't get the sense that my mother had an easy upbringing." Grandma DuBois barely acknowledged Sophie for most of her young life. Then again, she barely acknowledged anyone. She was widowed, old, and entitled, and she expected to be waited on every time she came to the Quinn household, her upper lip curling at most anything she didn't approve of. Except for Sophie's father, she seemed to like him. The parallels were evident.

"I'm working on a surprise for you." Brian's voice lifted as he said those words.

Sophie wiped the remaining tears from her cheeks and smiled. "Really? What is it?" Any surprises entering Sophie's world were rarely good ones.

Brian scoffed. "Well, I can't tell you that, silly. It wouldn't be a surprise now, would it? But I think you'll like it. I'm building it with my dad."

"Oooh. Intriguing. Is it a birdhouse?" She thought about their first encounter and the baby bird they had saved.

"You'll find out. And no more questions. Before I forget to mention it, my dad needs some help removing a stump from his backyard today. Do you want me to come by your place before I go? I told him I'd have dinner with him and stay the night."

*Aw, how sweet.* Sophie loved how Brian spoke about his father in an almost protective manner. She longed for that type of relationship with her parents. All she knew how to do was protect herself, mostly by hiding her feelings and her hopes and dreams. If you were invisible, no one criticized you.

"Wow, you're really embracing the yard work lately. How is the clearing going at Julian's place?"

Brian exhaled and answered, his voice deadpan, the way most people would sound facing a task they didn't enjoy. "It's going. That's all I can say. Want me to swing by and give my Soph a hug? Sounds like you've had a challenging morning."

*His Soph.* She *was* his. And she loved knowing that.

"Nah, that's okay. You go help your dad. Tell him I said hi." Sophie turned off the exit for Nellysford. In just a few minutes, she'd be back in her sanctuary. "Does he know about me? Your dad, I mean?"

Brian paused. "Yup."

That stirred all kinds of butterflies in her belly. Good ones. "Really? What did you tell him?"

"Not a lot yet. But I will."

And then a call came in on her CarPlay. "Hey, Brian, my dad's calling me right now." Her father's name illuminated her screen. "Can I call you back? Or better yet, we can just talk tomorrow. Good luck with your dad."

"Sure, Soph. I lov ... uh, talk tomorrow." *Click*, the phone disconnected.

*Love you, too.* They were both struggling to say those words out loud. But considering they'd only been together for a couple of weeks, she was okay with that. Even though she had told Brian a lot about herself, there were still things they didn't know about each other. Brian remained a mystery to her. She didn't even know where the guy lived.

The incoming call pulled her mind away from that thought process, demanding her attention. Time to pay the piper, so to speak. "Hi, Dad. Listen, if you're calling to give me a hard time about Mom, I'm sorry I slapped her. But she had no right to say those things about Charlie." Part of her worried that the slap-heard-around-the-Quinn-household would cause her mother to wash her hands of Sophie for good. As hard as Sophie's mother was to please, Sophie wanted her in her life. She was the only mother she would ever have, and that meant something to her. When she married Chad, things were better between them. She wanted that cease-fire to continue. If only she could convince Cecilia who Chad really was.

"Hello? Are you there?"

"Yes, I'm here. What did you say?" Sophie asked, sheepish that she had zoned out.

"I said, that's not why I'm calling. I felt like we blindsided you today, and I'm sorry about that. And I'll admit, I shouldn't have told Chad or your mother that you were coming to town. You had asked for a private meeting, and I should have respected your wishes."

"Who are you, and what have you done with my father?"

Johnathan grumbled. "Not funny, Sophie. I'm trying to be nice here." He paused for an uncomfortable number of seconds.

Not wanting to roll her window down and create interference on the line, she adjusted the temperature control in her car to accommodate her heated insides. As much as she loved the man, her father scared the shit out of her. "Was there something else?"

"Yeah, I'm on my way to your place. I know it's somewhere past Charlottesville, but you need to send me the address. I've cleared some time in my schedule for you. You wanted to talk to me, so I'm gonna give you the opportunity to do that. Fair enough?"

Sophie was so shocked that she almost forgot to answer. "Uh, yeah, that's fair. I'm not sure I have much else to say other than what I said earlier, but"—she took a moment to let it sink in—"thank you, Dad. I appreciate that."

"Splendid. Send me the address. I just left Richmond, so it's gonna take me a little while to get there."

The minute she got home she texted Brian. *My dad is coming. Holy shit. I'll text you later what happens.*

He responded immediately. *Good luck, Soph. I'm pulling for you.*

Brian had no idea how much his support meant to her. It wasn't something she took for granted. Having someone you could trust, someone who understood your plight, was an incredible feeling, and one she never wanted to go without again.

* * *

Pacing her humble cottage like a caged lion, Sophie decided to put on a pot of coffee. *What if he wants a drink?* She checked the time: 1:30 p.m. *Not out of the question, especially on a Sunday.* She pulled out her scotch next. *Did he eat at the brunch earlier?* Taking into account how quickly he and Chad had made it to the family home, probably not.

She went to work making pancakes, her stomach growling for food. The bacon came next, and then some scrambled eggs. By the time Johnathan showed up at her door, she had a full-on brunch going, the table set, and every drink available that her father could possibly want. It helped her to pass the time. She'd also sampled everything, which satisfied the rumbling echoes in her hollow gut.

She thought back to the few times her father had let his guard down. One moment stood out to her. It was right before her wedding. She and her dad were waiting in the Church's vestry for the organ to signal it was time for them to walk down the aisle. It was one of those rare instances when Cecilia wasn't around. Her father took her hand and stared lovingly into her eyes. *"I'm so happy for you, Sophie. Big day."*

She'd sighed and stared back at him, her heart brimming over with love. *"It sure is."* She brushed her hands down her gown, inspecting for wrinkles. *"Do you think I look okay?"*

Her father smirked. *"I think you look radiant."* Standing before her, he took both of her hands. *"I hope Chad makes you happy. You deserve all the happiness life has to offer."*

Years of invisible clouds dissipated between them and, for just a moment, the sun came out, casting rays of hope and love over their bond.

She shrugged one shoulder, a wave of bashfulness flushing her cheeks. *"Aw. Don't make me cry, Daddy, you'll smudge my makeup."* She ran a delicate finger under one eye that was threatening to tear up.

Johnathan didn't reply right away. Finally, he leaned over and kissed her cheek. "*I love you, Sophie. I may not show it, but you are the most important person in my life.*"

As Sophie returned her thoughts to the present, she placed a hand over her heart. "I sure hope you feel that way after I tell you the truth," she said to the empty room.

*Knock, knock, knock.* And then the doorbell. She'd heard his tires coming up the driveway.

Taking a calming breath, Sophie surveyed the buffet cluttering her island, along with the plates, the utensils, and napkins at the ready. With everything Quinn-worthy, she approached the door and opened it.

"Hello, Father. Nice of you to drive all this way out here."

Wearing a long, black overcoat and smelling expensive with a spice of class, Johnathan Quinn leaned in and kissed his daughter's cheek. Like Chad, Johnathan never had a hair out of place, his strong jaw and vibrant blue eyes, projecting strength and charisma. And the man was always wearing a suit. "You're my daughter, and I owe you an opportunity to explain yourself."

Sophie backed up so he could enter. And then she took his coat and placed it on the hook near the door.

"Smells good in here. You been cooking?" He gave her a sideways glance, his head tilted in disbelief.

She rolled her eyes. "Yes, Dad. I do know how to cook." Honestly, she was certain the man thought her an imbecile. She ushered him into her kitchen. "I wasn't sure if you'd eaten, so I made us a late breakfast."

The way his eyes glowed and his mouth watered told her she'd done the right thing. "Coffee?"

* * *

With full bellies, they sat at her kitchen table, sipping on their coffee, just like she and Charlie had. And just like she and Brian had, for that matter. She'd been having a lot of meaningful discussions lately. Hopefully, this would be another one. They'd covered the weather, the new house (she'd given him a tour), and her job. Now it was time to get real, judging by the way her dad was sizing her up.

"You don't love Chad anymore?"

She didn't hesitate. "No."

"When did you stop loving him?"

Sophie had been holding her mug, which she placed on the table. "I don't know, Dad." She thought about Brian and what real love felt like. Supportive love with mutual trust. "I don't know if I ever loved him."

Her father made a noise in his throat. "How can you say that? You two have been together since high school. It's been what, eight years?" He practically slammed his hand down on the table but stopped himself. "Is he messing around behind your back or something? I know I keep him busy, but I can't say I've ever suspected him of cheating or seen anything suspicious." Confusion and frustration flooded her father's eyes.

Few people caught Johnathan Quinn off guard.

"No, it's not that." Sophie held Johnathan's intimidating glare. "I thought you, of all people, would understand." She tried *not* to choke on her words. The man was scary when he wanted to be.

Johnathan jerked his head back. "What the hell is that supposed to mean?"

"Well, when did you stop loving Mom?" She crossed her arms over her chest, her chin raised in indignation.

Johnathan sat back in his seat as though her words had shoved him. "What?" He got all flustered. "Who said I stopped ... This isn't about me."

He was right. And if she had any chance of winning him over to her side, she needed to avoid another needless argument, even if he deserved one.

She leaned forward and placed her hand over his on the table. "You're right. We're not here for that. You asked if Chad was unfaithful. The answer is no, not that I am aware of anyway. But he has gotten abusive." Without her mother there to intervene, Sophie was braver with her honesty. She pulled her hand back. "I don't want to go into the details, but—"

"Abusive?" Her father's face got all tense. "Has he physically harmed you?" Johnathan's brow lowered like the shade of a window, dark thoughts clouding his eyes.

Sophie gathered up her courage like they were chips on a blackjack table in Vegas. *Now or never.* "Yes, he has. Multiple times. And more so lately. You don't know him, Daddy. He wants everything you have. And he feels like I'm standing in his way. He's threatened me, too. That little show he put on for you at the house"—she raised a finger in the air—"it was an act." Her palms hugged her coffee mug for comfort. "When you went out to take a call at brunch, he was much different with me." Her hand remembered the squeeze and the pain that followed.

"Different, how?" The muscles in her father's jaw flexed.

She could see his mind sorting through her accusations. Sophie stared down at her mug before she looked up. "Mean."

Johnathan's phone buzzed on the table, but he ignored it. He *never* ignored calls. "How long has this been going on?"

She swallowed the hardness of it all. "Well, there have been signs of it for many years, but things got worse just over six months ago."

"When you left?"

She nodded. "When I left."

"What kind of abuse? Did he shove you or hit you?" His eyes flared, enough that Sophie gulped.

"I'm not going to get into that. He's been abusive. And I don't feel safe living with him anymore. You have to believe me. I wouldn't say this if it weren't true." Her heart was beating like a jackhammer, her palms tacky. Whatever the result of this conversation, her father would know the truth. "I know he's your VP. And I don't expect you to fire—"

"He's out." He practically barked the words at her, his mouth twisted with disgust. "I won't have anyone abusing my daughter. I'll get you the best lawyer in town to divorce his sorry ass." He shot up and paced the room. "Son of a bitch." He rubbed his forehead. "Why didn't you tell me this?" He was huffing like a riled bull, his nostrils flared.

Sophie rose from her chair. She had never heard her father so angry. Were pigs going to fall from the sky next? Goose-bumps ran up her spine, making her shiver.

Johnathan raised a firm hand. "I'll take care of everything." He looked at his phone, his eyes surveying. "I need to get back."

She didn't want him to go. "Do you have to leave?"

All at once, Johnathan's demeanor changed. His angry eyes and red cheeks returned to normal. "I'm sorry, Sophie. I've got a big meeting this afternoon." He placed a hand on her shoulder. "Don't you worry. I've got this. I'll take care of everything."

The trouble was, she didn't want him to take care of everything. She wanted people to treat her like a grownup. A real adult. One who people took seriously.

She walked him to the door. "Thanks for coming, Dad. And thanks for believing in me." She wanted to smile but was too busy preventing her eyes from overflowing with tears. *If you want him to take you seriously, be strong.*

Her father looked down at her, his eyes softening. "I'm sorry this has happened. And I'm sorry you've had to go through this alone. You won't have to anymore." He placed his hands on her shoulders, the warmth from his fatherly love cascading around her like invisible snowflakes.

"Thank you. And I would like the name of a good lawyer, but I want to do the rest."

His head flinched back. "What? Why?"

"Look. I'm twenty-three years old. I need to stand on my own two feet. If I need help, I know where to find you. This is my life, Daddy. It's time I lived it."

This time, he smiled, something she rarely had the privilege of witnessing. "I'm proud of you, Sophie. You've become a very strong young woman. Your mother would also be proud."

Sophie made a face. *Are you crazy?* "I'm not so sure Mom agrees with you. But thanks anyway."

* * *

It was as if Mary Poppins had possessed Sophie as she danced around the house, cleaning up and humming to herself. For the first time in a very long time, her outlook was good, the forecast calling for blue skies and smooth sailing. She didn't want to get ahead of herself. She had a lot of work to do. And she knew she'd also have to deal with Chad, but her father was backing her. And as intimidating as Chad could be, he was no match for Johnathan Quinn, a man who could make or break careers with one word. Well, maybe a few more than that.

When the house sparkled, she went for a walk down the beaten path. She called Charlie as she strolled along.

"Hey, Poppy. How's my favorite girl?" A voice carried through from the background. "Is that Sophie? Give her my best."

"I'm good, Charlie. Really good. And tell Ginny, hi. I was just calling to let you know that I did speak with my father about Chad." A cloud floated over the sun, shading her walk and cooling the springtime air. Luckily, she'd grabbed a jacket in case, which she untied from her waist to put on.

"Oh, how'd it go?"

She laced her arms through the jacket sleeves. "Great! He's going to get me the name of some good lawyers, and he supports my decision to divorce Chad." A flock of small birds darted overhead, one chasing the other into the branches above, the woody aroma of the trees reminding her of Brian.

"Well, what do ya know? I'm heartened to hear it, Poppy. I knew he'd come through for ya."

Sophie let her eyebrows rise and fall. "Well, that makes one of us. I'm so excited. I get to stay living out here. And I get to see more of you and Ginny." Her tone turned snarky but in a playful sort of way. "Hey, when are you two gonna let me make you dinner? Ginny hasn't even seen my place yet. Or I can bring dinner to you. I'd love to see your house again now that you're all unpacked. We can sit out on your front porch like we used to do." Her thoughts returned to all those fond memories they'd shared. It also gave her an idea for a housewarming gift. A few Adirondack chairs with cushions. It would be perfect, and the stores would be stocked with summer furniture right now.

"That sounds good, Poppy. But you don't have to make us dinner." A light scuffle ensued, Ginny taking over the line. "Now, Sophie, you come here, and we will make you a nice dinner, ya hear? How about this Thursday? I'll make chicken pot pie, one of Charlie's favorites."

"But—"

"Now don't you go givin' an old woman a hard time. I'm makin' you dinner on Thursday, and that's the end of it. Can't wait to see you, Sophie. You can catch me up on your goings-on."

Sophie knew there was no arguing, so she didn't try. "Okay, but I'll bring dessert. I'll make chocolate cream pie since I know it's also one of Charlie's favorites."

"How did I get so spoiled?" Charlie had returned to the line.

"Because you are a good person, one of the best. So is Ginny. And you deserve it." Sophie's tone was firm but loving. "Hey, I gotta run. See you on Thursday."

After she ended the call, she tried Brian next, half expecting him not to answer, considering he was helping his dad with the stump. A voice mail wasn't ideal, but she wanted to deliver the good news as fast as possible. Unexpectedly, Brian answered on the first ring.

"Hey. What's up? I mean, how'd it go?"

"Great."

The sound of a paging system blared in the background, movement making a shuffling noise over the phone.

"Where are you? I thought you were working in your dad's yard."

Brian kept his voice low, which competed with the background noise. "We were, but my dad accidentally cut his hand, and I had to run him to the ER."

Sophie stopped walking. "Oh, no. Is he okay?"

"Yeah, he's fine. Just stubborn as a goat. He gave me a hard time about coming here. The cut was pretty deep. He needed stitches."

"Do you want me to come there? Which hospital are you at?"

"No, we're good. He should be out soon. We're picking up dinner before we head to his place. He wants me to watch some miniseries about the Civil War. He's been talking about it for weeks."

More voices carried into the phone from Brian's location.

"Okay. Are you sure? I could pick up some food and meet you at his house." She didn't even know where the man lived.

"Nah. We're good. But thanks, Soph. I may stay an extra night, just to make sure he's okay. He gets lonely, you know how it is?" Brian lifted his tone. "So, how did the meeting go with your dad ..."

* * *

With Brian out of town (although she wasn't quite sure how far out of town he was) and while she waited for her father to email her a list of lawyers, Sophie got a lot of paperwork done for her job. Mainly, what she did was review case files for the director of the nonprofit to see who would qualify for their services. Sometimes, she interviewed applicants to seal the deal. She enjoyed that part, getting to know these women and their stories. There were a few who just wanted a free ride, but most were sincerely looking for a new way of life. A leg up. And for those, Sophie wanted to give them everything she had.

When she broached the subject of teleworking on a permanent basis, her boss, Colleen, said she was okay with it but required that Sophie come to Richmond once every couple of weeks to meet and go over their cases in person. In fact, she wanted her there the next day.

"I'm going on vacation next week, and I'd like to go over anything that may come up while I'm gone," Colleen said.

It was a tiny office with only a few people working there, but Colleen said she wanted to cover all her bases.

Sophie agreed.

She spent her Monday night catching up with Brian. "It's gonna be a busy week. I've gotta drive to Richmond tomorrow for work, and then I'm having dinner with Charlie and Ginny on Thursday night." She wished he could join. *Patience.* And then an idea occurred to her. "Hey, if you ever want to stop by when I'm not here, maybe take a break from Julian's place, you're welcome to. I'll put a spare key under the planter just outside the front door for you. You know the one I mean, right? The one with the big fern?" She liked knowing that Brian worked so close. In fact, she'd started thinking about expanding her patio, just to keep him around *and* to contribute to his business. Brian didn't seem like someone who would accept charity, but she knew he'd accept good, honest work.

"I do. That's nice of you. How long will you be gone?"

"Just a day. But since I'm coming to town, my boss asked me to go to dinner with her. I'm not telling my family about it, though." Sophie couldn't imagine the hassle that would create.

She could almost hear Brian smirking over the phone.

"Can't say that I blame you there. Did your dad send the list of lawyer names yet? And don't forget, I can add to that list if you need me to."

"Not yet, but he will. He's a very busy man, but he was pretty adamant about it." Stretched out on her favorite sofa, Sophie sank into the cushions, her feet extended over the ottoman.

"Hey, how is your dad doing? How's his hand?"

"Fine. He's trying to adjust to doing things with a bandage on it. He's not supposed to get the stitches wet for the first forty-eight hours, and then he can shower. I'm helping him until then. Since you're not going to be around tomorrow, mind if I stay here another night? I've already cleared it with Julian."

Wow, the fact that he felt the need to ask her such a thing was major. "No worries. I'm gone on Thursday night, too, don't forget. Once the dust settles with this divorce, and I have an opportunity to tell them about you, I'd love to bring you with me sometime to meet Charlie and Ginny. They're awesome."

"I'd love to meet them when the time is right. There's no rush. We've got plenty of time for that."

*I didn't say I was in a rush.* Sophie also couldn't help but notice that Brian hadn't offered to have her meet his dad. She chewed on her lower lip. "So where does your dad live? I don't mean the address, but is it far from here?"

"Don't open that jar, *Dad*," Brian said to his father in the background. "Just let me open it. I'll be off in a minute." He huffed. "Like I said, stubborn as a goat. What did you ask me? Oh, I remember. He lives in Waynesboro, about forty-five minutes from you. I'll take you out here sometime."

That sounded promising. Her heart danced in her chest at the thought of it. She had never been more eager to meet someone's parents. Chad's parents were just like Chad. Or vice versa. They were cold and determined people. Sophie imagined Brian's father was much different.

Okay, now it was time to ask him the real question burning a hole through her tongue. "Where do *you* live? And when do I get to see your place?"

Brian sort of groaned as if not thrilled about having to answer that question. "I don't live in a nice place, Soph. I'd rather show you my dad's place." He chuckled in a bashful sort of way.

She didn't find the humor in it. Mainly because she really wanted to know more about this man. Their mutual love for each other seemed to come a step ahead of the getting-to-know-each-other phase. She wasn't sure how to date like this. "I don't care about that. I just want to see where you—"

"Dad! Don't open that. Jesus Christ. Just give me a ... Hey, I'm sorry, Soph, I've gotta run. Have a good day tomorrow and on Thursday with Charlie and Ginny. We can meet up on Friday night." Brian sounded so flustered. "You're gonna tear those stitches, old man." And that was the end of *that* call.

Sophie stared at the silent phone in her hand. Brian's private life was like Fort Knox, guarded and off-limits. Was that how all small-town men were? Did they grow up with so few people around they got used to the isolation? Or maybe he *was* an axe murderer, and he didn't want Sophie digging around into his dark past. She smiled at that ridiculous concept. For the time being, she was willing to be patient. But there would come a day when she'd want to know more.

True to his word, her father emailed her some names of lawyers, ones who he wrote could get the job done and fast. She needed a separation agreement. Either that, or she'd have to wait another six months for the divorce, according to Virginia law. Would she need a restraining order?

She spoke to her father about it over the phone. He seemed to be answering more often lately, something she had to get used to.

"Do you think I'm gonna have a problem getting Chad to sign the agreement? I want to make it fair for both of us."

Her father was firm. "If he wants a good reference from me and a generous severance package, he'll sign whatever you want. Either that, or he'll never work another day in this industry again. I'll see to it."

"Dad. I can handle this. Don't do anything. Maybe he'll sign it anyway. What did Mom say about it?"

Her father took a few seconds to answer. "Don't concern yourself with that right now. You need to focus on picking a lawyer from that list I sent you. Tell them who you are, and get that separation agreement finished. They all know me. Linda James is a shark in the courtroom. She'll take good care of you. Got another call coming in. Talk soon."

*Click,* the phone call ended.

"Linda James. I can do that," Sophie said to herself. She had a lot of decisions to make. Divorcing someone was a lot more work than she had anticipated. Did she want their house? Not really. She didn't even want any of the furnishings. They'd only remind her of Chad. She had her own home now, one she'd done a great job decorating. Two bedrooms upstairs and two bedrooms down, one of them a master suite. She didn't have a formal living room or dining area, but her breakfast nook, and her comfy living room provided just what she needed. What was even better was how safe she felt, especially knowing that Charlie and Brian were close. Hell, even her father was on her side. Hopefully, her mother would come around.

With that thought in mind, Sophie got up from the couch and headed for bed. After putting on her pj's and brushing her teeth, she jumped into bed, the blankets still offering remnants of Brian's earthly scent. She'd washed their love-making out of the sheets already but appreciated his aroma still remaining on the outer linens. She missed him and his furry whiskers.

Sophie startled awake, her eyes blinking open. *Was that a noise?* She waited to see or more accurately, listen. For nearly seven months of living alone, she'd gotten used to the solitude and the noises of the house, but every now and then, she'd have a night like this one, where she worried someone was in the house. It was silly, but it happened nonetheless.

*Bang.* And then a stumble, something sliding across the tiled floor. Oh, dear lord. Someone *was* in the house. And if her ears were correct, they were in the foyer. *Shit.* Her heart beat like a hammer against her ribcage, her lungs paralyzed. What was she supposed to do now? Hide in the bathroom? She grabbed her cell from the nightstand, her fingers frantic as she texted: *Brian, are you there? Someone is in my house.* Then she called 911.

A man answered. "Emergency."

"Someone is in my house." Sophie was frantic.

"Do you require police, fire, or ambulance?"

Footfalls drew closer to her bedroom door as Sophie slid out of bed, quiet as a mouse. It was like a horror movie, the sounds of footsteps coming closer.

"What?" Sophie was panting over the line. "I don't know. Someone is in my house." Carrying her phone with her, she crept to the bedroom door to lock it. Then the plan was to find her gun in her closet. Having a gun was a decision she'd made without hesitation. She lived alone, and she needed protection. Getting the gun was a no-brainer. She took the class, and she got the permit.

"Miss, where are you? Can you please give me your address?"

Her throat beyond dry, she struggled to speak as she whispered her address to the 911 operator, all while tiptoeing toward her closet. Her heart was beating so fast she was sure the intruder could hear it.

"Miss, I couldn't hear you. Can you please speak up? Is the intruder in the room with you right now?"

Another loud thump, and her bedroom door swung open, Chad stumbling inside.

She screamed, her body jolted with fear.

Chad grabbed her phone and slammed it to the floor, his foot shattering it into pieces. "So, this is where you've been hiding out?" Chad looked around in wonder, his words slurring.

Sophie's windpipe cut off all the oxygen she needed to scream more. Not that it would have done her any good. No one was around. "W-what are you d-doing here?" She should have gone for the gun first. Now, it was all the way across the room. She ran, only to have Chad grab her wrist like a vice to stop her.

"Where do you think *you're* going? Don't you know it's rude to leave your guest behind? I just got here, and I'm not done with you yet." His eyes red and glossy, Chad's breath brewed with alcohol. "I don't understand you. We had a good thing going." He bellowed, his voice echoing off the walls of her so-called sanctuary. "But then you went and fucked everything up."

# Chapter Ten

"C-chad. You need to leave. Right now! If my father finds—"

"Don't waste your breath. *Daddy* has already fired me." He rubbed his eyes, his footing unsteady. And then he stared at the floor, shaking his head. "I worked so hard ... so fucking hard." He flung a hand up and let it fall, slapping against his thigh. "I kissed everyone's ass until my lips turned brown." He pointed with a shaky hand. "I put up with you, *dearest*. And that was the real challenge." He thrust her up against the wall.

"Chad. Listen, I can talk to my dad. He said he'd give you a reference. You can work anywhere you want. And you can have the house and the furniture. You can have it all. Just please leave. I won't tell anyone you were here." Sophie tried everything she could think of to calm him down.

He stared right through her. "Bullshit. Thanks to you, I can't have everything I want, bitch. You fucked that up for me, remember?" He leaned in, his face all washed out with intoxication. "And all because you didn't like the way I fucked you? Don't act like you weren't a whore from the start."

Sophie could see he was winding himself up.

He braced both hands on the wall, flanking her head.

If only she could slide down the wall to her closet, she'd have a chance to defend herself. "I'm not a whore, Chad. You hurt me. You know what you did."

He pressed his body up against hers, his muscles rigid. "Shut up. Shut the fuck up." His breath was rancid, his eyes ferrel. "You are going to listen to me." He gripped both of her arms and flung her across the room and onto her bed.

She sprang up, ready to bolt in any direction available, but he was already there, waiting. "Fine. I'll listen to you. You haven't done anything that you can't recover from. I won't tell anyone you were here. Just please—"

"Silence! You don't get to talk right now. It's my turn." He loomed over her, his voice rocky and unstable. And then he grinned as though Sophie had just told him a joke. "You remember when I asked you to the prom in the eleventh grade?"

She nodded, her feet inching toward the floor.

"Don't. Move. I'm telling you. You don't want to defy me right now."

Could she take him? Could she push him out of the way? He was clearly drunk. But he was also bigger than her and in shape.

"Answer me!" Spit spewed from his mouth as he screamed at her.

She jolted. "What?"

"I said, 'Do you remember when I asked you to the prom in the eleventh grade?'"

She was flabbergasted. "Yes, I remember." Of course she

did. It was the happiest moment of her life until she woke up one day and realized her dreams had turned into a nightmare.

He tilted his head, his eyes mere slits, his body leaning over her like a thundercloud. "Didn't you ever wonder why a popular guy like me wanted to take a loser like you to the prom? You had no friends. No social life. My bros gave me so much shit about it. 'Why you taking Gollum to the prom, dude?'" Chad made finger glasses around his eyes as he continued to giggle to himself.

*Bastard.* Sophie always hated how large her eyes were. *Mila Kunis, my ass.*

"You know what I told them?" He placed his hand over his chest. "I said, 'Because her mother paid me to.'" He stared at Sophie as if waiting for that new development to sink in.

And sunk in it did, like an oil stain. All those years her mother had controlled her every move, who she hung out with, who she dated. She had orchestrated her marriage, too? If Sophie had any misgivings about the divorce, she didn't anymore. She'd be having a long talk with her mother about all of this. How dare she do this to her daughter? That was, if Sophie survived the night, her eyes zoning in on the broken door. *Can I reach it?*

"You know how many sympathy fucks I got in high school because of you? Shit, even the guys wanted to fuck me." He snickered to himself. "You were my charity case. Only you were a rich charity case. And that"—he raised his index finger—"made it worth my while."

He was being cruel, and she wasn't going to let him get to her. "Whatever, Chad. You're saying my mother paid you?" Sophie was fuming and afraid all at the same time.

"Oh, yeah. She paid me. And she said that if I would be your boyfriend, she'd make it worth my while. She'd make sure I was on the fast track with Daddy Warbucks."

Sophie's stomach was experiencing turbulent waters, the acids rising into her chest. She'd been prostituted out by her own flesh and blood. Did her father know? The only thing more grotesque than her past was the man right in front of her.

"And you know what's worse?" He paused for impact. "She's not even your mother."

*What?* A nuclear bomb went off inside Sophie's head. She couldn't fathom why Chad was saying this. "That's a lie. Please, just leave." She flew to her feet, only to have Chad push her back onto the bed.

He fell on top of her, his hands holding her wrists above her head. His breath was lethal, his eyes equally so. "That's right. Don't you ever wonder why Cecilia hates you so much?"

Sophie shook her head, her eyes clamped shut. "Shut up. It's not true. Leave me alone." Her voice wobbled. "Get out of here."

"I'll leave when I'm good and ready, bitch. And not until you know the truth. See, Daddy couldn't keep his dick in his pants. But you already knew that much. What you don't know is that he fucked some new maid who had started working for your parents. A pathetic whore. Just like you. And that whore got pregnant, like all whores do."

Shaking her head, Sophie tried to shut out his vile words that pierced her soul like poisonous arrows. "You're lying. It's not true. I don't believe you." She fought him to no avail. Once again, he had the high ground.

"The slut died during childbirth, and Cecilia decided to raise you, but only if your father didn't divorce her. You see, she couldn't have kids. So when she called you a street rat, she meant every word. You *are* a street rat."

Using all her strength and with a volt of newfound anger, Sophie thrust her knee up, making contact with Chad's gut. She wished she'd hit him right in the balls.

As he grunted and strained, she shoved him off her and ran for the door. She was just about out when Chad grabbed her hair and yanked, slamming her back against the floor. For several seconds, she struggled to breathe. He'd knocked the wind out of her. Her diaphragm spasming, she gasped for air.

While she fought to get her lungs working again, he straddled her, his knees pinning her arms like nails into wood.

"You fucking bitch." He grabbed her throat. "The last time I fucked you this way, I let you live."

"No, Chad. Please, don't. It's not too late for you. If you do this, they will know." Fear blanketed her soul in darkness. She couldn't see her way out.

He brought his face an inch from hers, spit from his mouth nauseating and vile. "You think I care about that anymore? You've ruined me. If he hasn't done so yet, your father will ruin me."

His disgusting voice cut through her courage like shark's teeth through flesh. She trembled to the point of quaking. She wanted to turn inward, fold into the fetal position, and stay there. This couldn't be happening. Her mind teetered on the edge of her sanity.

He'd lost it. Chad was out of control. And now he was going to kill her.

"Don't worry, dearest." He tightened his grip on her throat. "If you don't fight too much, I'll spare you."

Oh, God. The worst moment of her life was replaying all over again. The predator she'd married was going to kill her. But not before he raped her first. It took her until now to finally realize he'd raped her before. It wasn't a kinky sex game. It wasn't him experimenting. It was rape. Plain and simple. And he was about to do it again.

As if his ghastly face wasn't chilling enough, he opened his mouth and licked her neck and face, the saliva layering her skin in toxic waste. She'd die here. And she'd suffer before she did so. Knowing this fact, she fought hard, her knees kicking up, her feet flying every which way they could.

A shadow formed above Chad's head, an arm hooking around his neck. Suddenly, Chad flew back as if a rope had pulled him.

Gasping for air and trying to regain any sort of composure, Sophie realized the rope had a name. Brian. She sat up just as Chad flew across her room, his body doing a great job playing wrecking ball against her dresser.

Taking long strides, Brian grabbed hold of Chad's shirt collar. "You piece of shit. You like abusing women, do you?" He reached back and slammed his fist into Chad's head, then he shook his hand out, pain flitting across his face.

"Who the fuck are you? Listen, she's not who you think she is."

Brian's knuckles cracked against Chad's cheekbone, then his nose, red goo dribbling down his chin. "Unless you want to visit the morgue, you better get your ass out of here... NOW!" He flung Chad like a rag doll over by the door. "You ever come back here again, and I'll fucking kill you."

Injured and starting to sober up, Chad scampered to his feet, stumbling, as he raced for the front entrance, his body bouncing off the walls. A moment later, Sophie's monster was gone. A car's engine sounded off in the distance, its wheels skidding up the pavement.

Still trying to shake the shock out of her nervous system, Sophie attempted to stand.

Brian fell to his knees, his hands cupping her cheeks. "You, okay, Soph? Do you need a hospital?" He kissed her forehead. "I got your text, and I raced here." He exhaled as if he'd been holding his breath. "I'm so glad I got here in time. Did you call the police? He's going to jail for this." Brian examined Sophie's face, and then his gaze met her eyes. "Why are you looking at me like that? Why aren't you saying anything?"

What sort of rabbit hole was this? Sophie couldn't fathom what was happening. Her world didn't tilt right. The air didn't smell right. She struggled to speak, words unable to reach past her lips. And then, finally, she said what was cluttering her brain.

"Why is one of your eyes blue?" Glacial blue, to be precise. She knew the answer, and she didn't like it much.

Brian backed away and stood. "Uh." He turned away from her, but it was too late.

Sliding her butt across the floor and over to her bed, Sophie pushed up on the mattress to stand. "Answer me, Brian. Why is one of your eyes blue?"

He didn't answer. He just stood there like a tree, his head so bent it was about to break off. "I'm sorry, Soph."

Outraged, her insides twisting and turning like she was made of taffy, Sophie stood in front of him. "Sorry for what?" She pushed him and screamed. "Sorry for what?"

Brian closed his eyes, remorse dragging his face down. "I wanted to tell you."

The truth hit Sophie like a freight train, each car filled with more and more lies. "You *wanted* to tell me? You've been lying to me ... from the start?"

A ghost of a nod was all Brian would offer.

"You're Julian?" Her mouth lost all moisture, and her stomach felt like it was in one of those paint can shakers at Lowe's. She stared down at the palms of her hands in disbelief. "But. But I've told you so much about me. How could you not trust me enough to tell me this?" Her mother wasn't her mother. Brian wasn't Brian. Up wasn't up. "You're just a simple guy, huh?" Anger rode in like the four horsemen and up her spine. "Not much to tell, huh? You know what you are? You're a liar. And you're just like all the rest of them. You said your last name was Hughes. Did you just make that up?"

Brian rubbed his eyes and exhaled. "Hughes was my mother's maiden name."

For the first time since Brian had arrived, Sophie noticed his white T-shirt and lounge pants. She'd never seen him in anything but his work clothes.

Brian stood back, the chords in his neck protruding. "You want honesty? I'll give you honesty." His face tightened, his brow lowering under the tension. He lifted the sleeve of his T-shirt up over where a bandage remained a few days ago. Only no injury existed. "You see this?" He pointed to a tattoo. "You know what it is?"

Sophie stood there perplexed. It was a black circle with what appeared to be sunrays surrounding it.

"It's an eclipse. And you know why I have an eclipse on my arm?" He didn't wait for her to answer. "Because I wrote a song called "Sunshine." It was about all the women who I'd ... met once I'd hit the big time." He stared straight through her. "And I met a lot of women, Soph. The song was my pathetic way of thanking them for their time." He clenched his jaw. "Rebecca thought it was about her. It was what pushed her over the edge. That song. That fucking song ruined my life. And ever since then, my life has been one long eclipse."

Dangling at her sides, Sophie's hands turned to fists. "Not ever since." She stomped one foot. "*Not* ever since then!" Her voice weakened. "You met me. We found each other. We love each other." She wanted to finish with *right?* But she didn't dare.

This man wouldn't even look at her. He seemed to ponder what she had said.

Why did he need to ponder it? Wasn't he sure?

Finally, he shook his head, his chin sinking lower into his

chest. "I don't know." He dared to meet her teary gaze. "What I do know is that you don't want to be with someone like me. You deserve better than anything I can ever give you."

"What are you talking about? Why did you even start up with me?" She flung her hands out, her body wobbling like she had no bones. "Was it all a lie? Were you ever going to tell me?"

"I shouldn't have started anything up with you. I was wrong."

Were there any good people left in this world? Everyone was out for themselves. And Julian was no different. She could see he was hurting. He had closed the vault of his heart. She could feel that, too. What did *her* heart want? To shut down and build a fortress around itself, never letting anyone in. Yet somehow, a tiny piece of her resolve still wanted to try. And that tiny piece still wanted him to open up again and let her in.

"Did you ever love me?" She had to ask. She had to know.

"I already told you, I don't know. I don't think I'm capable of true love."

That was not what she wanted to hear. "But you said ..." She felt like a little girl begging for his affection. The pick-me girl.

Silence fell around them like a cold rain, the chill in the room unbearable.

Rubbing her face, Sophie was lost. Nothing felt right anymore.

"I didn't plan on meeting someone like you." His voice defied. "Goddamn it. I just wanted to be left alone." He spread his hands out. "Nothing good can come from this. You have no idea what it's like to have a gun pointed at your face." One blue and one brown, his eyes glimmered with painful tears. "You have no idea what it's like to be responsible for two women dying." His voice fell. "I'm no better than Chad. I fucked more women than you can imagine. I couldn't even remember their names, Soph."

Clamping her jaw shut, she spoke through gritted teeth. "Don't call me that. My name is Sophie. You say I have no idea what it's like to be you. Well, let me break something to you. You have no idea what it's like to be me. Ever been raped when someone is strangling the life out of you? Ever find out that your mother isn't your mother after all? And that the woman you had *thought* was your mother sees you as nothing more than a street rat? Apparently, my birth mother is dead." She thought about what her dad had said to her recently. *"Your mother would be so proud."* He wasn't talking about Cecilia. He was talking about someone else. Someone who Sophie would never have the chance to meet. She had always thought that Cecilia had hated her. And now she knew why. Given the fact that both Cecilia and Johnathan had blue eyes, and given the fact that the only thing she had inherited from her father was his nose, she was sure Cecilia saw the other woman every time she gazed into Sophie's oversized, hazel eyes.

She took at step toward Julian.

He took a step back, his palm raised, an invisible fence staking him off. "I'm sorry about what's happened to you. I really am. I want to help ... but I can't." He rubbed his eyes again. "I can't even help myself." He sounded so defeated.

"But *I* can help you. We can help each other." She wanted him to believe her. Of all the horrible things she'd just discovered, losing him was the worst.

He pulled his shoulders back and turned to face her, his eyes sending a clear message. "No."

This was a man who women sought after. He was used to the cling. He was used to women going batshit over him. She didn't want to be *that* woman. She'd been rejected enough. Her heart was as fragile as a thin piece of glass. Not only that, his eyes of two different colors told her all she needed to know. He was off-limits. To her and to everyone. And there was nothing she could do about it.

"Well, since you clearly don't want me in your life, please leave, Bri ... I mean Julian." Inside, she felt cold and desolate. "Just go." Her legs fought to remain standing.

His voice a mere whisper, Julian spoke. "I can't leave you here. What if he comes back?"

Sophie went to her closet and pulled out an object. A padded metal box with a combination lock. She punched in the necessary numbers and withdrew a gun. "If he comes back, I'll shoot him in the leg. I've already called the police. They'll probably show up ... or not, seeing the night I'm having." She'd never shot anyone before, but something told her she'd rise to the occasion.

"You know how to use that thing?" He stared at the gun, his eyes brewing with something Sophie couldn't identify. Alarm? Shock?

"I've been through training and have a permit to carry, so yes. Now go. Thank you for saving me. And thank you for keeping me company these past few weeks. You owe me nothing." She was so full of crap. This was not what she wanted. She was in love with him. And he was the first person she could say that about. Up until she'd met Julian, she'd been going through life with blinders on. And now she knew what real love felt like. But he didn't feel the same way about her. He couldn't even tell her who he was. She'd shared deep, dark secrets about herself.

"Soph—"

"Please, Brian ... or Julian ... or whoever you are." She placed a trembling hand over her forehead, her insides melting down, her heart doing its best to stay open. She wanted him to stay. She wanted him to love her, but she knew that wasn't possible. Not anymore. He'd made that perfectly clear. *And I won't beg.* She'd spent her life trying to win over her mother's affection and her dad's. Even Chad. What had they all done for her? Lied and caused her pain. "I'm giving you a pass. Take it. You're free. I know I can't make you stay, even if I really want to."

There was no point in reasoning this out. She knew the outcome. Julian wasn't really interested in her. She was an unexpected distraction. He never even came close to telling her who he really was. Everything was a lie. All of it. He spoke about Julian in the third person as if he were someone else. It was messed up.

Chad saw her as a pathetic charity case. Gollum. Her mother saw her as a street rat. Sophie didn't know who she was.

With his body slouched and his spine bent, Julian did as she asked. He never spoke another word. He never even looked in her direction. He disappeared like a ghost in the night. An apparition.

As the hours passed, she wondered to herself, *was he ever real?* Sophie wasn't sure anymore.

# Chapter Eleven

As the sun crept over the horizon, Sophie shook her head out of the stupor that had governed her thoughts. Chad hadn't returned, and it had been hours. Without a working cell phone, she emailed her boss that she couldn't come in today. Luckily, she'd never called in sick before, so her boss was understanding.

Chad was bold, and he was relentless, yet it still surprised Sophie when he sent her an email bright and early.

> I fucked up. I was upset. I didn't want to lose you. Don't tell your father what happened. I won't contest the divorce. Please, Sophie, I was drunk. I didn't mean any of it. I wasn't going to hurt you. You can have anything you want.

The rest was just more rambling. He knew he'd destroyed her phone, so he was reaching out to her another way. And he was panicking. He'd have to be to expose himself like this. Now, she had proof. Sort of.

"Good, you bastard." She enjoyed seeing him squirm, even if it was only in writing.

The police never came. They must've not kept her on the line long enough to trace the call. Rural areas were a challenge for many reasons, emergency services being one of them. She'd learned that from one of her true-crime podcasts.

Sitting at her kitchen table, Sophie looked at her gun placed in front of her and pondered her life. What life? She'd gone twenty-three years believing one thing, only to discover none of it was real. Of course Chad could have been lying, but she knew he wasn't. She'd felt the distance from Cecilia for years. The ire. She just never understood what it was about.

She regarded her laptop. Should she email her dad? Or Cecilia? She didn't have the strength. There was nothing they could say. She did, however, think of two people who might just care that Sophie's world was spinning out of control. Charlie and Ginny.

Sophie showered, forced a few bites of toast down her throat, and made herself a coffee to go before she set off.

A handyman lived up the road, according to the sign in the yard. Sophie stopped there first to see if the man could repair the lock on her front door, enough to get her by until she had a security system installed along with a better door. From what she could surmise, it was mostly the casing that was damaged.

Not much was working in Sophie's favor as of late, but this guy, who turned out to be a woman (she'd served in Afghanistan as a mechanic and knew her shit), was free and had the door fixed within the hour. It didn't hurt that Sophie paid triple her fee.

As she drove toward Charlottesville next, her mind was a mixture of emotions. She realized she'd always felt different from the people around her. She never really felt connected to any one person or thing. (Charlie and Ginny were the exception.) She mourned for a mother she never knew. What was she like? Did Sophie's father love her? Or was it just as Chad had described: a piece of ass for a man who couldn't keep his dick in his pants. Nothing more.

As she pulled into Charlie's driveway, the clock on her dash flashed 7:30 a.m. She cut the engine and sipped her coffee, watching for signs of life coming from within the house. Knowing Ginny's recovery and need for rest, she refused to put her problems ahead of theirs. After a while, her eyes grew heavy.

"Poppy, is that you?"

Sophie startled and wiped the sleep from her eyes.

Wearing an old gray T-shirt and a pair of long, cotton plaid pajama bottoms, his hair a mess (what was left of it), Charlie approached the car, a layer of gray whiskers coating his chin.

Sophie opened her door. "Good morning. I didn't wake you or Ginny, did I? I tried to be quiet."

"You know me, Poppy, I'm up with the chickens. And Ginny's making coffee." He seemed to survey her for a moment. "You okay? Something wrong you want to talk about?"

Her lower lip twitched as she did her best to blink back the tears. "Can I come in?"

"Of course. Of course." Charlie draped his arm over her shoulders. "You come on in, and we'll make you something to eat." Just the tone of his voice set her mind at ease. She was with someone who truly cared about her. Charlie was her unicorn.

*  *  *

"Are you sure you've had enough to eat?" Wearing rollers and an old-fashioned housecoat, Ginny hovered over Sophie like a mother bird. She'd made pancakes with bacon for her.

Sophie's appetite wasn't good, but she ate the delicious food anyway since Ginny had gone to so much trouble to make it. It wasn't only the lumpectomy that had made Ginny's right arm so sore. They had removed her lymph nodes, which caused her a great deal of pain. Against Ginny's protest, both Sophie and Charlie helped her cook.

"I'm stuffed, but it was delicious, Ginny. Thank you. And let me do the dishes." Sophie stood, only to have Ginny shut her down.

"I won't hear of it. Charlie can help me."

Charlie nodded his approval.

Ginny placed a warm hand on Sophie's shoulder, guiding her back to her seat. "Weren't you coming for dinner on Thursday night?" She and Charlie exchanged a look.

"Yes, I was. I mean, I am. I'm sorry to drop by like this. I just didn't know where else to go." She bowed her head, the palm of Ginny's hand caressing her hair.

"You are welcome anytime. Now, I'll get started on the dishes while you tell us what's wrong, dear."

"Okay, but let me wash, and you can dry." Sophie sprang up, making her way to the sink before Charlie could beat her to the punch.

Having something to do with her hands would help the nervous twitch running through her fingertips like electricity. Sophie would have to be careful about what she shared. She didn't want to incriminate Chad just yet, not before she thought through how she wanted to handle things. She had Chad right where she wanted him. If he *had* raped her, things would be different. But thankfully, he hadn't. And the taste of freedom was close. "Cecilia isn't my mother, is she?" She hoped Ginny and Charlie could shed some light onto this very difficult subject. They'd been around a lot longer than Sophie had. *They had to know something, right?* Either way, Charlie wouldn't lie to her. She knew that much.

Ginny nearly dropped the pan she was drying, the metal clanking against the side of her porcelain sink, which Charlie, standing close, grabbed out of her trembling hands. He set the pan aside as Ginny wiped her hands with a dishtowel.

"Here, let's sit down." Sophie guided Ginny to the table, where Charlie joined them, his mouth hanging open, his face pale.

"What makes you ask us that, Poppy?" Charlie stammered as he wiped a hand across his brow.

Sophie tried to read their expressions. Wide eyed and slack-jawed, they looked like they'd both just seen a ghost. Ginny covered her mouth with her arthritic hand.

Sophie must've sounded crazy. Either that or ... *No.* She shook the thought from her head.

"Someone told me." Sophie raised a palm. "I don't really want to get into all of that right now. But I learned that Cecilia isn't my mother. And that my biological mother died during childbirth ... having me." Sophie felt awful about that part, even though she knew it wasn't her fault. "Apparently, my father was having an affair with this woman. And after she died, Cecilia agreed to raise me, but only if my father wouldn't divorce her." Sophie focused on the sky carpeted with gray clouds outside the kitchen window. "Poor woman. I guess she worked for them at our house. I'm guessing she was young and beautiful, and he took advantage—"

"No!" Charlie's chin trembled. "He loved her. And she loved him."

Tears spilled from Ginny's eyes.

Sophie watched them. "What's going on? You knew?" *Please, please, please, don't let me down. I can't take losing anyone else in my life.* Her insides felt as if someone had stuffed them into a blender and pushed the button for high speed.

Charlie nodded once, his tone somber. "We knew." He took Ginny's hand, giving it a gentle squeeze. "If she hadn't died, your father was going to divorce Cecilia, and they were going to raise you ... together." He stared at the wall behind Sophie. "But then she died, and everything fell apart."

By now, Ginny was sobbing.

Sophie ran to her side. "Ginny. I'm so sorry. Why are you crying? I didn't mean to upset you." Was she making them think of Justine? Was she drudging up old heartache? And then the truth slapped her in the face. She stared at Charlie and Ginny, both of them sobbing. This was personal. All the puzzle pieces that represented her life fell into place. How much her dad looked out for Charlie. How he paid their medical bills and even gave Charlie a pension. It all made sense now. Charlie wasn't just a gifted gardener. He was family. And so was Ginny.

"It was Justine, wasn't it? She didn't die from a heart condition. That's what you all told me, so that I wouldn't know the truth. Justine was my mother." She looked at Charlie's big, round eyes and then at Ginny's hazel irises. It was all there right in front of her.

And the fact that neither Charlie nor Ginny objected gave her the answer. Sophie fell back on her butt, the realization drowning her in a tidal wave of shock.

Now, it was Charlie's turn to run to Sophie's side. Ginny hunched over the table as if her heart was breaking all over again.

"Poppy. Please come sit." Placing his hands under Sophie's armpits, he lifted her to stand, guiding her back to her chair. "We knew, yes. But we had to keep this secret. Cecilia threatened to make trouble for us." He took a stabilizing breath. "He left her, you know."

Sophie didn't know how she was still managing to sit upright. Her body felt as stable as hot wax. Her heart wasn't sure whether to shut down or explode. Even her eyes had trouble focusing. Her father left Cecilia? Sophie tried to imagine that. The three of them, Justine, Johnathan, and Sophie, living happy lives. It was too surreal.

"When he found out Justine was pregnant, he started divorce proceedings. But Cecilia left the country, and he couldn't track her down. When Cecilia returned, Justine had already passed. Johnathan was distraught. He didn't know what to do. We tried to intervene, but Cecilia stood in our way. She even threatened to force your father to put you up for adoption. Your dad wanted you close to him. We all knew Cecilia could cause trouble. He did what he thought was right. But he loved our Justine. And she loved him." Standing close, Charlie placed his hand, rough from hard work, on Sophie's arm. "Your father kept me working all those years so I could be close to you. He has taken good care of us. He's paying Ginny's medical bills."

"No, Charlie, we should have told her. She is our grand-daughter. She is our own flesh and blood. We should have adopted her ourselves."

Charlie's hand went to his wife's shoulder. "You know that Cecilia would have caused problems for us, Gin." His gaze found Sophie again. "We did what we thought was best for you, Poppy." He bowed his head. "I'm sorry if we made the wrong decision." Tears ran down his cheeks, tearing Sophie's heart in two. "We've loved you since you came into this world, and we will love you until we are gone."

Sophie recalled all the special times they'd shared, the birthday parties, the holiday celebrations that her father had invited them to, despite Cecilia's grumblings. The moments she watched Charlie mowing the lawn and how comforted that had made her feel. She'd had them with her all along. A lot of people had made selfish decisions on Sophie's behalf, but this wasn't one of them. These people loved her. Truly loved her.

She rose and grabbed Charlie into a bear hug. Ginny, rising from her chair, joined them a moment later. "I love you both so much. Thank you for staying close to me all these years. I couldn't ask for better grandparents." The three of them stood huddled, crying their hearts out. They cried for the moments they had missed as well as the ones they had embraced. They cried for each other and for the love they felt. Sophie knew this just as she knew the sun would rise in the east and set in the west.

* * *

After Chad's attack and Brian's secret revealed, not to mention an emotional reunion with her grandparents, Sophie was beyond exhausted. Ginny made her a bed in their one guest room, which Sophie was all too willing to take advantage of. With the scent of lavender and vanilla bean coating the sheets and several pieces of antique furniture keeping her company in the modest-sized room, Sophie dozed off with a sense of peacefulness that she'd only experienced with one other person. Brian. She knew his name was Julian. But Brian was the man she loved. Julian was the man who couldn't love her back. If only she had her cell phone to tell *Brian* about everything that had happened.

Maybe it was for the best.

She'd lost Julian, or maybe she never had him to begin with. Just like Sophie, Julian was lost in a sea of despair. Would he ever come up for air? That wasn't something Sophie could control. He had his father, and that was at least something. Either way, he'd made her feel things she'd never felt for another man. Love. She knew this because it was different. Julian showed her what a real man was like, and she'd never settle for anything else again.

She let that thought comfort her as sleep overtook her mind.

* * *

The weight of someone's body pushing down on the bedsprings at the edge of her bed caused Sophie's eyes to flutter open. She rubbed her eyes and sat up, sunlight filtering in through the room's sheer curtains. She expected to see Ginny or Charlie, but it wasn't either of them. It was her father.

She wasn't angry with her grandparents. They did what they thought was right. But she *was* angry at Johnathan.

"What are you doing here?" She kept her tone tight and to the point.

His suit jacket and tie off, Johnathan had rolled the sleeves of his white dress shirt up toward his elbows, two buttons loose near his neckline. For a guy like him, that was about as casual as it got.

"I'm sorry, Sophie. I should have told you the truth long before now."

Sophie crossed her arms over her guarded chest. "But you were afraid of Cecilia." Sophie coated her voice with ire, and she didn't care.

He shook his head. "I have no one to blame but myself. My mistakes are my own." He moved his hand out to touch her leg but pulled it back. Showing emotion wasn't something he did, not with her. "I wanted you close." He pursed his lips. "After your mother died, Cecilia agreed to raise you as her own. I kept

Charlie and Ginny nearby." He stared down at the floor. "I did what I thought was right for everyone, especially you."

Sophie unlaced her arms. She swung her feet over the side of the bed to touch the floor. "You should have told me, Dad. You robbed me of my grandparents for over two decades." She was fuming.

"Not true, Sophie. They've been right here with you. I made sure of it. Even though you didn't know who they were, you still kept them in your life." He paused as if to gather himself. "There is something else I want you to know." His blue eyes softened in a way that Sophie had never witnessed. "I loved Justine. I was going to marry her. And we were going to raise you together. Fate had other plans." He reached back and pulled out his wallet. "I keep this with me everywhere I go." He pulled out a tattered picture of Sophie and showed it to her.

"That's me."

Johnathan shook his head. "No, that's your mom."

Sophie took the photo from his hands. Staring back at her were those same big hazel eyes and long black hair. The resemblance was uncanny. Only *her* features looked positively radiant. "She's beautiful."

"*You're* beautiful, Sophie, and every time I look at you, I think of her. She was a special young lady, and if you can ever find it in your heart to forgive me, I'd love to tell you more about her."

Damn it. She was angry. Why did he have to say that? The trouble with anger was it only hurt you. She handed the photo back. "I forgive you, Dad. I just need some time." Something else occurred to her. "What will you do about Cecilia? The secret is out now. Will you stay with her? I know you two aren't happy." It was like *War of the Roses* with those two, an older movie that she happened to watch one day when she was flipping through the channels.

Staring off, Johnathan rubbed his jaw. "I think your mother and I." He exhaled and focused his eyes. "I'm sorry. Old habits die hard. Although, she is still your adopted mother. And I believe she does love you. Putting that aside, I guess I sort of checked out after Justine died. I let Cecilia raise you. Even though she is a bear of a woman, I knew she'd look out for you. My business was taking off. And I'm ashamed to say I just let things go. But she and I do have some things to work out."

That was hard to believe. It seemed to Sophie as if her adopted mother had spent her life punishing instead of loving. "But she wasn't good to me. She bribed Chad to go out with me. And then Chad abused me. It was her fault. She knew he'd hurt me. She saw the bruises. She won't admit it, but she did." Sophie was so angry about it all.

Her father's brow tensed. "She *bribed* Chad to go out with you? And she knew about the abuse?" He rubbed his jaw pensively, his eyes absorbing it all. "Cecilia and I are due for a long talk. And that will be happening very soon. I've let things go on for far too long. I can see that now. There's no excuse for her behavior ... or mine."

A smirk slid across Sophie's face. "If you're planning on kicking her ass, can I come?" She wasn't serious. In fact, she dreaded the talk she and Cecilia had in their future.

Johnathan rose to his feet. "There'll be no ass kicking. And I think it best you avoid this one."

Sophie stood as well. She went to hug her father, but realized who he was. A man who rarely showed affection.

He reached his arms out and beckoned her with his hands. "Come on. I promise I won't break." He grinned with that charismatic smile of his. The one saved for CEOs and now his daughter. After their hug, he stood back, his eyes turning serious. "I'm sorry I pulled away all these years." He ran a hand down the side of her head and hair, his voice wavering. "You look so much like her." His eyes filled with all the love his heart could hold, a tear threatening to fall from his lid. "I won't make that mistake again."

Sophie fell into his arms. "Does this mean you're going to start being around more?"

Her father exhaled, ruffling the hairs on the top of her head. "I'm sure gonna try."

Whatever was happening in Sophie's world, things appeared to be changing for the better. Without a very powerful secret wedged between them, father and daughter had nothing to stop them from expressing what Sophie had always longed for. His love and support. If only Brian ... *Nope, not going there.* A new family would have to be enough.

* * *

Sophie waited until Saturday to make her trip to central Virginia. Well, she'd already gone into work on Thursday, but that was to help her boss prepare for her upcoming vacation. She'd also used that time to get herself another cell phone.

She didn't get any more emails from Chad, but once she got her new phone up and running, a ton of voice mails from him begged for her attention. She listened to one: "Sophie, I'm sorry about the other night. I was drunk. Things got out of hand. Please don't tell your father. I'll go quietly. I'll do anything you want. And I won't bother you again. Some of it's a little cloudy, but I remember saying some things that weren't true. I was just spouting off. I love you, and I was hurt that you wanted to divorce me. Don't take anything I said to heart. I didn't mean any of it." He was practically stuttering. "Please, just don't tell your father. Send me the papers, and I'll sign. Anything you want."

Some part of her still enjoyed hearing him squirm. That

bastard had put her through so much hell already. And things could have gone so much worse. What if Brian ... She shook her head. *Stop calling him that.* What if *Julian* hadn't come when he had? Things would have been much worse. Even if Chad hadn't tried to kill her, he was clearly set on raping her. She'd never forget that look in his eye, that hatred for her. On the other hand, she'd gotten what she wanted. She'd be free of him. She would even save all of his communications as her insurance, which she would also make sure he knew about when the time was right. She sipped her coffee, the dark liquid providing necessary caffeine to her brain cells, the bitter taste coating her tongue and throat.

She'd spent all of Thursday evening with Charlie and Ginny, poring over pictures of Justine, each one sparking a memory that both Charlie and Ginny shared with her intermittently. Of all Sophie's kitchen-table discussions, this was by far the most special. Justine was high-spirited. Justine was smart. "She made honor roll every year of high school." What Sophie learned the most about was how kind her mother was. "Once she got her own apartment and the job with your family, she started volunteering at the local animal shelter." Pride colored Ginny's words as she placed her reading glasses, attached to a thin chain around her neck, onto her nose. She flipped through pictures as she spoke. "She'd take in strays all the time." Her expression saddened. "After she left us, we took a few of the cats in ourselves." She held Sophie's hand tight. "Made us feel like we were helping, you know?" She nodded subtly.

It was surreal to hear about this woman who had made Sophie. In her parents' eyes, she was perfect. And Sophie was sure Justine went out into the world feeling special and loved. As a direct contrast, Sophie went out into the world feeling the complete opposite. Cecilia had always made her feel less than.

Other than marrying Chad, Sophie had never measured up in Cecilia's eyes.

She longed for a mother's love, never knowing quite what that kind of adoration felt like. To feel special. To feel like no one else on the planet could possibly measure up to you. She'd seen those mothers in movies and on TV. She'd just never experienced that kind of unconditional love for herself. Motherly love. The very moment when she was supposed to meet her mother, she was taken away from Sophie. And it was all her fault. Sophie was angry at herself for something she had no control over. Could it be another reason why her father was so distant with her all those years?

"Did she want me?" Sophie couldn't help but ask. "Or was I an unexpected surprise that ruined her life?" Tears spilled from her eyes. "I'm sorry she died having me." Her heart ached with sadness, her soul mourning this very important loss.

Both Ginny and Charlie surrounded Sophie with their arms and their love. "No. That was not your fault. That was God's choice," Ginny said. "We told you the truth about her heart. We didn't know she had a defect. It was very rare. And when she went into labor, her heart failed her. The doctor said it could have happened when she was running or doing any type of physical exercise. But what a gift she left behind."

When Charlie and Ginny pulled away, they both smiled, their eyes glimmering like sunshine sparkling off the waters of a calm sea. "Did she want you? She had never wanted anything more," Charlie said, Ginny placing her hand over her husband's arm. "When she found out she was pregnant, she was overjoyed. And believe it or not, so was your father. He was a very different man back then." He quirked an eyebrow. "Not as into suits as he is now."

"Anyway," Ginny piped in, "your mother loved being pregnant. And she wanted to name you Sophie right from the start."

"Why? What is the significance of Sophie?"

Ginny puffed her chest out. "Well, you just so happen to be talking with Virginia Sophie Walsh, thank you very much." She giggled. "It means wisdom."

Sophie's skin tingled. She was named after someone she adored.

As that fond memory faded from her mind, she had to focus on the other mother in her life. She'd been doing a lot of soul-searching when it came to Cecilia. It was easy to remember all the bad times. The summer camp from hell, the limited number of friends that Sophie was *allowed* to have. And the worst was Chad. But she also thought about the times when Grandma DuBois came to town, the constant disapproval she bestowed onto her daughter. For weeks, Cecilia would stress over her mother's visit, trying to make sure the food, the guest suite, the itinerary were perfect. It was the only time Sophie saw Cecilia vulnerable. And what did Grandma DuBois do in return? Disapprove of most anything in her path. Cecilia would work with the staff to serve a five-course meal fit for a king, and her mother would thank Sophie's father for his effort. Just like Sophie, Cecilia was invisible in her mother's eyes.

She'd take all of that into account when she saw her, which, according to the clock on Sophie's dash, was ten minutes from now. She'd called ahead to set up the meeting.

Soft, puffy clouds with a charcoal edge cluttered the sky as springtime in Virginia acquainted itself with summer, the air collecting moisture and heat. Sophie chose a sensible pair of tan designer capris with a sleeveless white cotton top and flats for her feet. She wanted to be as comfortable as possible for this *uncomfortable* conversation.

When she arrived at the family estate, no one was out front to greet her other than a gardener who was pruning some bushes. It gave her a few extra seconds to collect herself before facing whatever was coming. She couldn't help but admit she was nervous. Cecilia had been like the Great Wall of China to her. Impenetrable.

The moment she closed the enormous mahogany and stained-glass door, the scent of something delicious reached her nose. Something sweet. And then Cecilia appeared, her hands clasped in front of her, not a hair of her blonde bob out of place. Her makeup was perfect, and she wore a light-gray pencil skirt and a tailored white blouse to complement her sleek body. A pair of three-inch Prada mules with crystal embellishments adorned her feet. Like Sophie's dad, Cecilia always over-dressed. "I had lunch made for us out on the terrace. And for dessert, we made that apple cider coffee cake you like so much."

That explained the delectable aroma in the air. She'd made one of Sophie's favorites. Did she dare hope it was a good sign?

Those cold blue eyes of her adopted mother had lost some of their chill. But not for long.

"Is that *acceptable* to you?"

There was that edge.

Sophie sighed. *Well, I guess Cecilia's leopard spots haven't changed all that much after all.*

"That's fine." Sophie wasn't giving anything away, her emotions remaining in check. She loved Cecilia. She was her mother. But she didn't need her anymore. And that changed the rules.

* * *

With their napkins folded in each of their laps, adopted mother and daughter sipped sweet tea as the waitstaff brought out Caesar salads at first, then braised chicken salad, and apple cider coffee cake with candied pecans for dessert. Sophie couldn't wait to dig into that one. For several minutes, they ate, so they didn't have to talk.

"Lunch was delicious, Moth—" Both Sophie and Cecilia froze, the awkwardness between them as loud as a sonic boom.

Exhibiting perfect manners and grace, Cecilia dabbed the corners of her mouth with her cloth napkin and rested it on her place setting. "I know you hate me for what I did. And I know you don't think of me as your mother anymore ..."

Sophie leaned in. "But?" She wasn't offering any branches, olive or otherwise. Not yet.

Cecilia seemed to shake out her nerves, but it came off looking like a snub.

Sophie remained quiet. She wanted to give her the benefit of the doubt.

"But I did what I thought was right for you."

This was where she lost Sophie's patience. What was right for her? Nothing about her life up until now had felt *right for her*. She shook her head from side to side in amazement before she dropped her napkin on the table as though it were a microphone. "How was setting me up with and making me marry Chad right for me? And how was keeping the secret about my birth mother right for me?" Sophie's cheeks smoldered, resentment engulfing her feelings. "You hated Charlie. And if it were up to you, I never would have known him."

Her arms crossed over her chest and her head tilted to the side, Cecilia waited as if counting the seconds to continue. "Are you done? Do I get to speak now?"

Sophie blew out her lips. She motioned with her hand. "By all means, *Cecilia*."

Her adopted mother closed her eyes for a moment.

Did Sophie's refusal to call her *Mother* strike a nerve? If it did, then good. She deserved it.

Cecilia uncrossed her arms. "First of all, I thought Chad

would be good for you. You seemed to be floundering, and he came from a good family and had a bright future, all the things I wanted for you." She fiddled with the diamond stud in her earlobe.

Sophie wanted to pick up her empty plate and smash it on the ground. She didn't, mainly because it wouldn't be Cecilia who'd be picking it up. "I had friends at one time. But you forbid me from seeing them. I even had a boyfriend, remember?"

Cecilia shook her arrogant head. "Collin?"

Sophie was surprised she remembered his name.

"Do you want to know where Collin is right now?" She leaned over the table for impact. "He's in jail for robbing a convenience store with a gun." She waved a hand in the air. "Is that the kind of future you wanted for yourself? I knew that boy was trouble." Using her index finger, Cecilia poked the table-cloth. "I was looking out for you. And just so you know, I did some checking into Chad's family. He had good parents. If he turned out to be abusive, that's not on me. He always seemed so well-mannered when I saw him."

A scoff flew from Sophie's lips. "You paid him to take me to the prom. You bribed him to be my boyfriend. How did you think that was going to go?"

"When I approached Chad to take you to the prom, I did offer him money, but he refused to take it. He said he liked you and wanted to do this on his own. He said he'd already been thinking about it." Cecilia crossed her arms again as if to say, *your move.*

"That's not what he told me. Did you know he and his friends called me Gollum behind my back? Does that sound like a guy who had feelings for me?" Sophie's hand slammed down, making the dishes rattle, and her mother jolt. "And he was abusive. I told you that, but you didn't believe me."

"Well." Cecilia's resolve was waning, her eyes showing worry. "I didn't know that."

"You did know. You saw the bruises on my neck." Sophie's lunch was starting to thicken in her stomach, her chest uncomfortably hot.

Cecilia stared at Sophie as if she had just grown three heads. "What in the blazes are you talking about? What was wrong with your neck? And when did I supposedly see *that*?"

"Almost seven months ago. Remember? We went to lunch, and you were going on and on about your stupid drapes? I had bruises all over my neck."

Her adopted mother seemed to contemplate that. She lowered her voice. "How was I supposed to ..." Pursing her lips, she took a moment to regroup. "I don't remember anything of the sort." She primped her haughty bob.

*Fine.* Sophie couldn't prove that she knew. Unless Sophie could read Cecilia's mind, which she couldn't. Regardless, Cecilia wasn't fessing up. And Sophie had more questions. "How did Chad know our little family secret? Did you tell him?"

Cecilia set her jaw. "I most certainly did *not* tell him." She huffed.

"Then how did he know?"

Cecilia shook her head subtly. "He's helped your father with a lot of legal work. He must've gone through some of our papers and found something."

"How did he know that you couldn't have kids?"

The revelation caused Cecilia's eyes to widen. Her cheeks flared. In fact, a sheen of sweat formed on her brow. Finally, she exhaled. "He told you about that?"

Sophie nodded. She kept her eyes glued to her adopted mother. What was happening?

Cecilia sat back in her chair, her stature sagging. "I was

unaware that he knew. He must've found some of our medical files." She stared off for a moment, and Sophie actually felt bad for the woman. To not be able to have children had clearly hit Cecilia hard, the invisible wounds still very fresh.

So, Cecilia hadn't told Chad. They weren't the team that Sophie had suspected they were. Sophie could easily see Chad going through their files with a fine-tooth comb, looking for something on her family. He was like that. He'd found out some dirt about a professor in college and used it to get an A in a class he was failing. Sophie had discovered this one night after they had graduated. She'd overheard Chad bragging about it over the phone to one of his bros, a few glasses of scotch influencing his loose lips. He didn't know she was home at the time, and they never spoke of it.

She could accept Cecilia's answer. Moving on. Sophie had more axes to grind.

"First, you took off overseas so my father couldn't divorce you, and then you only agreed to raise me because you probably didn't want to lose him. Or maybe you didn't want to lose your standing in society. You bullied him while he was grieving into staying with you. And you kept my grandparents from telling me the truth. You wanted to put me up for adoption. What kind of person does those things?" She glared across the table. "A selfish bitch, that's who."

Her voice weak, Cecilia answered. "Your biological mother died during childbirth. I had nothing to do with that. I went overseas to clear my head. I was devastated. And, yes, I did want to put you up for adoption. At first. But I couldn't have children, and I grew to see the benefit of having you around."

"Yeah, you saw how it benefited you, not me."

*Is she tearing up? Oh, this is too much. And the Oscar goes to ...*

"How would you feel if the man you loved had an affair

and wanted to leave you for another woman?" Cecilia's hand shook as she dried a few tears with her napkin. "My mother always told me to find a man who could take care of me. When I couldn't have children, she acted as though it was all my fault. I tried. I did everything I could to get pregnant." Her voice grew despondent.

It was like watching a statue crumble before Sophie's eyes. Her adopted mother's resolve cracked, creating fissures throughout the glacial wall of her convictions.

"And then I found out Johnathan had gotten someone else pregnant. Yes, I was angry. He left me for her. She was young and beautiful. She was everything that I wasn't. I had failed. I couldn't go back home. My mother would never let me live it down." She took a sip of her tea, her voice normalizing. "I'm not proud of some of the things I've done, but I did raise you." She pointed a defiant finger. "I kept you safe and out of trouble. And I didn't know that Chad was so abusive. Yes, I was firm with you, but my mother was firm with me. That was the only way I knew how to parent." Her voice faltered. "And you look so much like *her*." Cecilia turned her head away, her gaze falling to the floor.

As Cecilia's defense rested, Sophie sat back in her chair and let it all sink in. Mistakes were made. Too many to count. But it wasn't all bad. Sophie did have a home. And she did have her dad, not to mention her loving grandparents around her as she grew up. She also realized something else. What Sophie had always wanted from her adopted mother was something that Cecilia didn't have the ability to provide. It was like trying to get water from a dry well. She was cold, but she wasn't without regret. Cecilia regretted a lot from what Sophie could see.

Her voice calm, Sophie reopened the floor. "Let me ask you something." She waited for Cecilia to meet her gaze. "Did you ever love me? I mean, really love me, like a mother would love her daughter?"

Cecilia swallowed as she adjusted herself in her chair. She took a breath and gazed out over the back lawn, where the over-sized swimming pool and tennis courts lived. "I loved you as much as I was capable."

Well, at least she was honest. For once.

"You know my dad is going to leave you, right?"

She nodded. The corners of her mouth crimped downward.

Another round of silence swallowed up the air between the two women.

Sophie pushed her chair back, the wrought iron legs scraping against the patio pavers. "Thank you for lunch. The cake was delicious." She rose and grabbed her purse off the back of her chair.

Cecilia shrugged one shoulder. Her eyes remained sad. "I knew it was your favorite."

Sophie released a pent-up breath. It was so hard for her to stay angry. Cecilia was the only mother she ever knew. And she loved her, blemishes and all.

She approached her mother. "There is nothing we can do about the past. We can only move forward." She placed a soft hand on Cecilia's shoulder. "And if you want to have a relation-ship with me, you'll have to make the effort. And you'll have to accept Charlie and Ginny as family. Those are my terms. No more lies. No more manipulation. I'm staying in Nellysford. And if you want to see me, you'll have to come to me." Sophie removed her hand. "I do love you, but I'm gonna need some time before we can get to that point."

Cecilia stood and straightened her blouse. "As you wish."

# Chapter Twelve

The next two weeks crawled by, Sophie keeping up with her job and visiting with Charlie and Ginny as much as possible. She also had a new door and an impressive security system installed, which she should have done from the start.

One night, she hosted a dinner with her grandparents. Steaks on the grill and baked potatoes with salad. She invited her father, and he came. And to Sophie's surprise, he wore navy pleated shorts and a white polo, no socks and loafers. Wonders never ceased. At first, the conversation was stiff and superficial, but as the subject of Justine continued to make its rounds, he opened up about her. That was something that Sophie had hoped for.

The foursome sat on Sophie's back patio around a large table with a small fireplace at its center. The setting sun cast ribbons of peach and lavender across the horizon, the mountain range taking one last yawn before bed.

"Once Justine had started working for us, I began noticing her walking dogs near the animal shelter in Richmond. I was intrigued by whose dogs they were and stopped to chat with her about it." Johnathan's eyes glazed over as if the past had consumed his thoughts. "She told me about how much she wanted to help the pets at the local shelter, and she even convinced me to take a dog in. A bichon frise. Cute little thing." He ran his fingers across his lower jaw. "He had thick, wavy black fur with a cluster of white fur around his mouth. It looked like a beard." His gaze found Sophie. "You remember Duke, don't you, Sophie?"

She did remember. "We got Duke from Justine?" She'd loved that dog, even though Cecilia hadn't. In fact, Cecilia wouldn't let him anywhere near the formal rooms in their house. If Duke needed food, she wasn't going to feed him. If Duke needed bathing, Sophie or one of the staff had to do it. If Duke peed on the floor, his backside felt the end of her rolled-up newspaper or magazine. *I think she even kicked him once.* But looking at this from another angle, she did let the dog stay. Cecilia was a paradox, one that Sophie would take years to figure out.

"Gosh, he died, what? Fifteen years ago?" Sophie asked.

Her father nodded. "He was a good dog."

"I remember him running around the yard," Charlie said. "I didn't know that Justine had convinced you to take him in." He chuckled. "After she passed, we took three of her cats. It was as if she was telling us what to do from the grave. In this world or the next, I swear that girl could talk anyone into just about anything."

The four of them shared a moment of laughter, even Sophie's dad, who said, "She sure could." His eyes glowed with what Sophie knew was lost love.

It was hard for Sophie to accept that she had missed out on all of this. There was nothing she could have done about her mother dying during childbirth, but she missed learning about her father's past as well as her grandparents. Even not knowing who they were, she'd loved them anyway. And she still had time to love them some more. She let that nice thought nestle into her heart.

With all of these good vibes blessing her life, the days still crawled by like cold molasses. Sophie kept watching *Entertainment News*, hoping a new segment would come on about "Where in the world is Julian Sommers?" That was a question that Sophie would really like to know the answer to. She knew where he lived and the iron fence that surrounded his castle. Hell, it was just up the hill. But he might as well have been a thousand miles away. A couple of times, she broke down and texted him, always asking the same question: *Are you there?*

He never responded. His silence was deadly. To her heart, anyway. Maybe he'd already moved on. Maybe he was relieved that things had ended. He was a kind man. And she was in love with him, but she also knew you couldn't force someone to love you back. He'd only said those precious words once that she could remember and *almost* once over the phone. And they'd only been together for a few short weeks. It didn't matter that, to her, it felt like a lifetime.

The following week, Sophie finished her separation agreement, Chad compliant about everything. They decided to sell their house, and Chad moved back to Georgia near where his family had moved several years ago.

When she got restless, Sophie walked, her heart always beating at twice its normal rate when she passed by the place where they'd saved the baby bird. The place where she'd met the love of her life.

"Helloooo."

A voice called out from behind her. Was it Julian? She steeled herself, her lungs straining to breathe, her balance starting to sway as if she had suddenly come down with a bad case of sea legs. Finally, she turned as a middle-aged man (about the same age as her father) approached, wearing a loose pair of olive-colored shorts and a plaid, short-sleeve, buttoned-down shirt. His gray hair was thick and wavy, a few lines creasing his face. His eyes, however, were a perfect match for Julian's. Glacial blue. Sophie's favorite color.

Wearing hiking boots with thick, dark-gray socks, he carried a walking stick. The man could have modeled for Eddie Bauer. "You wouldn't happen to be Sophie, would you?" He wiped a sheen of sweat from his brow. "If you aren't, do you happen to know where she lives?"

"Yes, I'm Sophie. Do I know you?" Of course she didn't know him, not formally. She was floundering with what to say next.

The man stopped and rested his weight on his walking stick. "My name is Brian Sommers. I believe you know my son, Julian." He reached his hand out to which she shook, his smile reaching all the way to his eyes. "I was hoping we could talk for a bit."

*Brian?* So that was where he'd come up with the name. "Uh, sure. How is Julian?" It felt so strange to call him that, as if she were talking about someone else.

Brian nodded as though the news was good, or maybe he was just being polite. "He's ..." Then he seemed to reset himself. "Julian is in North Carolina right now." Brian furrowed his brow as if not sure of himself. "Would you have a few minutes so we could talk?" He pointed over his shoulder. "We could go to Julian's place or yours. I don't know exactly where you live, but I know it's close." He paused and watched her with cautious eyes.

"Is everything okay?"

Brian hesitated to answer. Instead, he readjusted his walking stick and changed his footing.

"Sure. I mean, of course. I live just over there." Sophie pointed toward the direction in which she had come, and the two of them made their way there.

As they walked up her driveway, she pulled her house key from the front pocket of her shorts. "How is your hand? Bri ... I mean, Julian told me you had cut it pretty badly."

Brian turned his right hand over, a raised pink scar drawing a line across the lower portion of his thumb. "Good as new. Just need to be careful when I'm sawing wood." He smirked.

Sophie was on pins and needles, curiosity burning like a wildfire in her chest. Stomach tight, she tried to tamp down her nerves. Hoping her hands didn't shake, she unlocked her door and punched in the code for her alarm while Brian turned his back to her, probably to give her privacy. The scent of crème brûlée welcomed Sophie back home from several air fresheners infusing the air. She inhaled a calming breath, then asked. "Would you like something to drink? Water, perhaps?"

Brian leaned his walking stick against the wall near the door. "Water would be great, thank you." His gaze traveled the house. "Nice place. Did you decorate it yourself?"

The duo walked toward Sophie's kitchen. "Thank you. And, yes, I did. I love it here." She filled two glasses with ice and water from the door of her fridge, her eyes seeking out the Blue Ridge Mountains past her kitchen window. "Here you go." She handed one glass to Brian and motioned with her free hand. "Let's go sit out on the back patio. It's still nice and shaded right now." Carrying her glass with her, she guided Brian through the French doors and onto her back patio, made of limestone, doing her best to make a good impression. She'd always wanted to meet Julian's dad. She just never expected him to come to her.

She took a seat, and Brian did the same, both of them facing each other. "So, what did you want to talk to me about?" She was dying to know.

Brian took a generous sip of his water, then placed the glass on the table and smacked his lips. "I understand that you and Julian were friends, but you aren't seeing each other anymore?"

Sophie nodded, not happy with that acknowledgment. "Did you know that Julian told me his name was Brian?"

Brian offered a somber nod. "I suspected as much."

"I didn't know who he really was." She looked away. "I guess I should have suspected, but he wore brown contact lenses." She made a fluid motion with her hands near her head and chin. "His hair was so long, and that beard covered most of his face. I didn't consider that he was anyone other than who he said he was." He was bigger, too. She'd double-checked that video of him performing on stage. Two years of isolation and yard work had built Julian's muscles to a whole new level.

"Yeah. He got pretty good at hiding his true identity. He even wore those contact lenses in the house. It was as if he couldn't stand looking at the real Julian in the mirror." Brian exhaled. His face was drawn with worry. "Well ... I'd like to try to explain my son a little better and what he's been going through these past couple of years." He scratched his temple. "When that poor young woman killed herself and Julian's companion, he went into shock for a time." A layer of sadness washed over Brian's eyes. "You know about that, right?"

"Yes, I originally saw the story on TV." Sophie was happy she was helping Julian's father get this out, not an easy thing to do, judging by his strained speech and wary eyes.

Brian exhaled as though relieved he didn't have to explain it all again. "Yes, well, as I said, Julian was in quite a state of shock. After he met with both families and helped them take care of the funeral arrangements, he had nothing left to accomplish. He didn't get out of bed for a month. And then he wouldn't speak for another two months. He just stared off into space." Brian's cheeks flushed pink. "It was hard to watch him fade away like that. Julian lost his mother a long time ago. Since then, it's just been the two of us." He lowered his chin. "I didn't know what to do to help my son. I called therapists, and they came out to meet with him, but he wouldn't participate. I called on a cousin who Julian was close to and his manager and agent, but he wasn't interested in talking with anyone about what had happened."

Sophie angled her head, her heart reaching out to the man. "I'm so sorry, Brian. That must've been awful for you."

Brian took another sip of his water. "It was worse for my son. He was lost. You see, he'd always been gifted musically. And he had a voice like an angel. Got that from his mother. She used to sing all the time." He smirked. "Not me. I can't carry a tune to the mailbox and back. *My* voice makes dogs howl for mercy." He half giggled. "But Julian was different. He knew back in grade school he wanted to play music. He joined the band in high school, played the piano and the guitar. Started his own band outside of school. Couldn't get enough of it." Brian sat back in his chair with his gaze reflective. "I wanted the kid to join the Marines like I had, but he wasn't built for that. And growing up without a mother, the boy deserved a good life, one that made him happy." His gaze settled on Sophie. "I don't expect you've heard him perform, have you?"

"I did look Julian up once online, after I'd been watching a story about the incident on TV. Julian had told me about it himself. But he said it had happened to his *friend*, Julian, not himself, who I had thought was Brian." She was glad he had confided in her but, at the same time, she felt horrible about his torment. "He also told me about Rebecca's family and how they had tried to take advantage of Julian. He said Julian had blamed himself for what had happened." Was she even making any sense? She'd entered some sort of warped reality. "Anyway, I watched a few minutes of him performing on stage. He sounded great." *And he looked great, too.* "I can see why he was so famous. He's very talented."

Mr. Sommers' eyes grew wide. "He talked to you about all of that?" A wrinkle deepened between his eyebrows. "He never talked to *anyone*, including me, about his feelings or what had happened." He rubbed his chin, his eyes taking it all in. "Wow. You must've been really special to him for him to open up like that."

Sophie's insides got all fuzzy, mainly because he'd told her quite a lot about what had happened and Julian's struggles with it all—*and* on more than one occasion. She wondered if talking about it as if it had happened to a third person had allowed Julian enough distance from the story to open up. Or maybe she had put a magic spell on him. Illogical as it was, she liked to believe the latter.

Sophie had worked through it all with him, providing another perspective. *"Keep talking sense to him. Eventually, you'll get through,"* she'd told him. Had *she* gotten through? It didn't seem that way anymore. Was what they had shared between them just a temporary blip on his screen of torment? Had he come up for air only to sink back down?

A sigh wafted from Brian's lips, bringing Sophie back to the moment. "It was two years of hell. And it continued to be hard until about five weeks ago, when he went for a walk to stretch out his back from leaning over his deck all morning. Several minutes later, I watched from the window as he grabbed his ladder from the side of his house and took off down the hill. When he returned home, it was as if a chatterbox had stolen my son. He told me all about the bird you two had saved. He must've mentioned your name half a dozen times." Brian ran his hand over the top of the table. "He had that spark that I had remembered seeing in his eyes, the one that I had thought was long gone." He raised both palms. "I tried not to make a big deal out of it. Didn't want to draw attention and have him withdraw again."

Sophie remembered the moment when she'd made Julian laugh. Knowing what his life had been like, it was a miracle. Somehow, she knew something profound had happened between them, even then. The memory of Julian traipsing over to her with his ladder in hand, half of the mountain glued to his backside, made her smile. And then he kissed her. Everything about their meeting was exactly as she had suspected. And she understood this without knowing who Julian was or what his life had been like. She was escaping her abusive husband and a family who made her feel invisible. Julian was escaping two years of darkness. And somehow, they'd found each other. Their powerful connection didn't care that they had only known each other for a short time. When something was right, you knew it. And they both did. Too bad it was temporary.

"A few days after he met you, he came home one night madder than a red hen, slamming around the house like a bull in a china shop."

Julian's dad liked clichés, and Sophie thought it was endearing.

She also remembered that night. The night he'd kissed her for a second time. The night he'd made the mistake of touching her neck. She'd freaked out about it. Threw him right out of her house.

He shrugged. "I didn't dare ask why. I just let him be. I figured anger was still better than what I'd been seeing over the past two years." He met her gaze again. "And then you came to his house several days later." He cringed. "Sorry I was rude to you. I got used to keeping the public out."

"Oh, so that was you on the intercom? I wondered." Sophie

placed her elbows on the table and let her cheeks rest over her fists. Hearing this story from another perspective was riveting.

"Yeah, that was me, and I'm awful sorry I was rude. I could see you both out there talking, and then you took off, and Julian came storming back to the house. I'll never forget it. He walked up the steps to his front porch, took one look at me, and said, 'Dad, your son is a self-centered prick.'" Julian's dad grinned. "I asked him why, but he wouldn't say any more than that. He took off that night and didn't come back until the next morning." He lowered his chin and peered up at Sophie from under his brow.

Sophie blushed, the night of their lovemaking fresh in her mind.

"All of a sudden, my son was a different person. He still worked on his house." He lifted his index finger. "And even a project for you, but he also started writing again and trying out a few chords on his guitar and his piano. My son's heart was beating again. And I suspect you had a hand in making that happen. When you called him, he was almost giddy about it. *Sophie this, and Sophie that.* 'Did you know that she helps less fortunate women find jobs, Dad?'" He shook his head in amusement. "He was like a schoolboy. Even at the height of his career, no one had made him behave that way." Brian's smile washed away, a dense fog encapsulating his enthusiasm. "And then, a couple of weeks ago, he dashed off in the middle of the night. When he came home, that distant and reclusive son had returned."

Her heart throbbed like a toothache. She knew why Julian had withdrawn. His secret was out, and Sophie was angry about it. The emotional scene between them must've set him back. *Big time.* "I feel terrible about this, Mr. Sommers. Julian came here to help me. You see, I've been separated from my soon-to-be ex-husband for seven months now. And he was abusive. He broke into my house that night and attacked me."

Brian sat up in his seat. "Good, God. Did he hurt you?" His eyes showed concern.

"He tried, but Julian came and stopped him. And as I said, up until then, I had thought Julian's name was Brian. I didn't know who he really was." She took another sip of her water, hoping to replenish her dry mouth and throat or maybe to wash away the lump that was forming. "I'm sorry, Mr. Sommers. I had no idea." She shook her head, flabbergasted by it all. "In the scuffle with my ex, one of Brian's brown contacts came out. I was angry that he had lied to me. We argued. And he said that I was better off without him."

It was easier for him when he was pretending to be someone else.

Sophie hated admitting this. It was an awful moment in her life. One of the worst. And considering she was married to Chad, *that* was saying something. "I tried to reason with him, but I could see he'd already built a wall up between us. And I'm pretty sure he doesn't want to see me anymore. I've texted him a couple of times, but he hasn't responded." If only Sophie was more secure with herself, she'd have tried harder. Those old wounds from her childhood were still very real. And she definitely had trust issues.

Brian pushed his chair back and stood. "This isn't your fault. And I don't expect you to do anything about it. I just wanted to try and understand what had happened. I got my son back, and then I lost him again. I also think he may be planning a trip."

"Oh?" Sophie stood, her stomach tightening. "What makes you say that?" She walked with Mr. Sommers through the house toward the front door.

"He's buying an RV, but he hasn't told me why. And I saw

some maps on his desk in his study of the Southwest and Alaska." Brian picked up his walking stick. "Even though he won't talk to you, I know he still cares about you. And I don't mean to alarm you, but I think he's been watching your house."

That didn't alarm her. In fact, she was touched. "Why do you think that?" She opened her front door for him.

"He had a few trees cut down in front of his house. I assumed it was to get a better view. And he bought a really nice telescope. Again, I thought it was for the view or the stars at night." Brian stepped out into the Virginia sunshine, a few crickets chirping from the lawn. "But then the other day, he looked through it and said, 'Good, she got a security system.' When he walked away, I peered through the scope, and what I saw was this house." Brian expelled a breath. "I didn't know it was your house, but I guessed as much." He reached his hand out again. "Thank you, Sophie, for talking with me. I'm sorry my son lied to you about who he was. And I'm sorry about all the trouble. You're a good person. I can see why he enjoyed spending time with you."

A handshake felt way too formal for the occasion, so Sophie stepped closer and offered a friendly hug. She made sure not to cling or linger, but she wanted him to know she cared enough to show it.

Since he was holding his walking stick, Brian hugged her back with one arm before he pulled away. "Yes, well, you have yourself a nice day."

He took a few steps down the path leading to her driveway when Sophie called out.

"Mr. Sommers." She ran over to him as he turned to face her. "Could we keep in touch about Julian? I'd like to know how he is. And if you think it would help, I could try talking to him again." She refused to beg, but she could at least try to reach out to him, considering the man had captured her heart. She hated that he was *Julian* now. It made her feel more self-conscious, knowing his past with crazed fans and endless women. Long-haired Brian, with simple clothes and modest means, was much easier to work with. Did she even know Julian? In reality, she was in love with a dream. Then again, her whole life felt that way, especially lately. It would take time to sort out all of her feelings. But she was up to the task. More now than ever before.

"Sure." Brian fished his cell from his front pocket. "Let's exchange cell numbers."

The next few days were agonizing. When the weekend hit, Sophie was walking the path three times a day. She texted Brian, who informed her that nothing had changed. And then, on Sunday night, Sophie approached her house from yet another walk to find a small package on her porch. She grabbed the envelope and sat right there on the stone steps to rip it open.

Inside, a short note awaited:

Dear Sophie, I'm sorry I lied to you. I'm sorry about a lot of things. I wish I could go back and change what happened two years ago, but I can't. It left scars that have changed me. What I feel for you is real. I want you to know that. And I hope this song shows that to you. It wasn't easy to write, but I owed you that much. I hope you have a good life. You deserve nothing *but the best. I wish that it could be with me, but it just can't. I've left for Alaska for the foreseeable future. I don't know when I'll be back. If you haven't done so already, move on with your life. Get the divorce from Asshalf and be happy.*

*You will always be the woman who made me laugh and, for a short time, put the sun back in my heart.*

*Love, Julian Brian Sommers*

With tears streaming down her cheeks, Sophie dashed into her house and over to her laptop, where she stuck the flash drive Julian had included in the envelope into the necessary slot. On it, an MP3 file stood by waiting for her to open, which she did a millisecond later. She pulled her cell phone from her front pocket so she could sit comfortably and listen.

"This song is dedicated to my Soph. It's called 'Sun in My Heart.'"

The sound of Julian's voice made Sophie shudder. It felt like years since she'd heard him speak. It was both welcoming and devastating. Her heart wept, her insides trembling as she sat there trying to breathe.

An acoustic guitar filled the room with a most beautiful melody. And then Julian sang to her.

> *I met you on a path*
> *When I was alone*
> *And then you made me laugh*
> *And my cover was blown*
> *You touched my heart*

*And I didn't know*
*That I'd made a new start*
*Even though it was slow*

*Sophie, it's you*
*And no one else*
*Who made me feel new*
*And less of a mess*

*You knew me as Brian*
*And I scared you at first*
*But soon I was trying*
*In spite of my curse*
*I'm sorry I hurt you*
*But I hurt myself more*
*Because I already knew*
*You had made my heart soar*

*Sophie, it's you*
*And no one else*
*Who makes me feel new*
*And less of a mess*

*You gave me a chance*
*You helped me belong*
*And for all that romance*
*I give you this song*
*I love you, Soph*
*And right from the start*
*That is no joke*
*You're the sun in my heart.*

A few more strums, and the song wound to its end.

By now, Sophie was sobbing, her head in her hands. How could he do this to her? How could he give her this song and then leave? She didn't know she could love someone this much. And she didn't know she could hurt so much from losing him. She slammed the laptop closed, her heart breaking and then rebreaking all over again.

"You son of a bitch!" She jumped up and ran out of her house, her feet determined to take flight. When she reached the spot where Julian had come sliding down the hill with his trusty ladder on that fateful day, she climbed, her hands digging into the soil, her feet sliding out from under her as she struggled to gain footing.

Covered in dirt, leaves, and God knew what else, she reached the top, where she brushed herself off and stormed toward his house like a human earthquake. At the hill's edge, she inched her body between the fence and a large rock, trudging toward the front.

Yes, he was gone, but the anger within her required an outlet. Either that, or she'd meltdown from the inside out. Why hadn't Brian told her Julian had left? Maybe Julian had asked him not to. As she rounded the side of this enormous house adorned with stone and ample amounts of glass, she tried not to fawn. Decks were everywhere, benches and fire pits galore, an oversized hot tub off to the side dove into the ground, stone accents tricking the eye into believing nature had made it herself.

*Nope, don't care.*

When she reached the front, the house looked deserted. No RV, no truck, no cars of any sort. The yard was cut. The landscaping was impeccable. A stiff breeze cooled the sections of Sophie's tacky body, and she leaned into it. When she was ready, she found center stage on the stone walkway leading to the stone front porch, and then she unloaded, her hands clenched by her sides.

"How dare you write me that song. How dare you leave me to pick up the pieces of my heart." Every muscle in her body was tense, her pulse raging. "You are a coward, you know that?" It was as if her chest was on fire, her stomach riding like a roller coaster up into her throat. "You tell me you love me, but you don't love me. If you did, you'd have the balls to stay here with me and fight ... for us." *You said you're no better than Chad. Well, you're right about that, too.* Emotions fought their way in, making her voice quiver. "I loved you when I thought you were Brian. I didn't care who you were. I let you into my life." *I don't do that easily.* "And now you're gone." She started to weep, her resolve melting away like an ice cube in a glass of steaming hot water. *And I'm afraid I'll never have the courage to open my heart again. That I will never trust a man enough.* "I deserved better than this! I deserved you."

That was it. Anger and frustration moved aside for the hurt and the emotions that ran down Sophie's cheeks like a raging river. Her body slumped, she took a step toward home. Until a voice rang out, stopping her in her tracks.

"You're right. You do deserve better."

# Chapter Thirteen

Once again, Sophie steeled herself. *Holy Shit!* She hadn't expected him to be here. Could it mean what she hoped it meant? *Don't put yourself through that.*

She spun on her heel and faced a gorgeous man with shoulder-length hair, a groomed chin, and eyes that could guide her through life's worst storms. She adored those eyes almost as much as she adored the man wearing them. No more work pants. His T-shirt was just tight enough to show off his chiseled abdomen, his khaki shorts riding low on his hips.

Trying to gain her composure, Sophie placed a flustered hand on her hip, her pulse thrumming in her ears. "I thought you left." She couldn't help but feel slightly out of place around this man, who looked so different from *her* Brian. This new, famous guy was breathtaking. If she was being honest, she was embarrassed that this stranger had seen her naked. Seen her? He'd devoured every inch of her body. Maybe not her neck.

Julian took a timid step forward. "I wanted to leave." He

pursed his lips, his eyes searching for the right words, or so she hoped.

"What stopped you?" Even though Sophie looked strong, she wasn't. One wrong word, and he could destroy her. Again.

"Well." He took another step closer, now ten feet away from Sophie. "My dad, actually."

Sophie's brow lowered. "Your dad?"

Julian nodded. "Uh-huh." He rubbed his jaw, the pads of his fingers acquainting themselves with his bare chin. "I finished the song I wrote for you last night. And after I played it back, my dad came into my studio."

*You have a studio? Focus.*

"He asked me if that song was about you."

Sophie hung on his every word.

"And I told him it was. He said that only once in his lifetime had he ever felt that strongly about a woman. My mother. And then he said that I couldn't control what had happened two years ago, but I sure as shit could control what happens now. He placed his hand on my shoulder, and then he added, 'I've met her, son, she's worth the gamble.'"

Shell-shocked, Sophie was speechless. "He said that?"

With love sparkling in his eyes, Julian took another step closer, his body less than a foot from hers. "He did, and he was right."

She looked around. "Is he here? And where is your RV?"

A smile spread across Julian's face, something she appreciated more now than ever. He made a cringy face, coupled with amusement. "Well, he took my RV hostage. He said he wasn't bringing it back until I spoke to you in person. He said no son of his was going to take the coward's way out." A tiny laugh glided from his lips.

"How did you know I'd come?" Because it was like he'd been waiting for her.

He gazed down at her with soft eyes, his hands lightly touching hers. "I didn't, but after I dropped off that letter, I watched your house through my telescope. I saw you read the letter and then run into the house. I assumed to listen to the song. Your song."

*My song?* That had a nice ring to it.

"A few minutes later, you bolted out of the house, and I knew where you were headed." His tone lightened with a tinge of humor. "You left your front door open, by the way, so I'm guessing the security company is probably trying to reach you."

She patted her pockets. No phone. In all the chaos and heightened emotion, she must've left it on the table. And then she pivoted her thoughts. "Oh, so what? You think making a joke is going to get me to love you again? You think shaving and cutting your hair, and"—she took several shallow breaths, flailing one hand in the air—"looking all gorgeous is going to win me over?" She narrowed her eyes and poked him hard in the chest. "Let me tell you something, *Julian*. I happened to love Brian. He made me feel things I'd never felt before. He changed me. And *you* didn't want me to know Julian. You didn't trust me enough." It was his lack of trust that had hurt her the most.

His voice soothing, Julian ran his hand down her arm, and she shivered. "I know. But it wasn't you that I didn't trust. It was me." He shook his head, his face pained. "I thought my life was over two years ago, and ever since then I've been only surviving. Day in and day out. Until I met you." With her hair locked in a ponytail, Julian brushed a few loose bangs out of her face. "When I met you, it was as if I had suddenly woken up. Like my mind had been in a coma. And there you were, standing right in front of me. You made me laugh, but there was something else." He angled his head, his gaze washing over her face. "I still don't know what it is.

All I can say is that every time I look at you, I feel alive again."

She wanted to believe him more than anything, but could she? That young girl who was left out in the cold emotionally didn't dare trust.

His arms wrapped around her waist. "I love you, Soph. And I have never loved anyone this much before. If you'll have me, I'd like nothing more than to spend the rest of my life proving that to you." He planted a few soft kisses on her forehead and then her cheek.

"What if you change your mind?" Sophie's inner demons were making her angry. If only they would shut the hell up.

"I won't."

"But we've only known each other for a short time. It was so sudden." And she had so much to tell him about.

He offered her a reassuring smile. "Yeah, well, when it's right, it's right. A few weeks or a few hundred weeks, love is love, no matter how long it takes. And you know how I know?"

Gazing up into his entrancing eyes, she shook her head. "How?"

"It's *because* I know. And I've never *known* anything this powerful in my life. I've met a lot of people, but I've never met you, Soph."

Okay, that was it. She was a goner. And thank God for that. Her resolve was hanging on by its fingertips. A grin slid across her face, one filled with delight. "You realize, I can't call you Bri anymore."

He pulled her hips against his, a rather large bulge pushing back. "You can call me Bri, or you can call me Jules." He placed his palms on both sides of her cheeks. "Just don't call me asshalf. Deal?"

She kissed his shaven chin. "Deal. And you'll always be Bri to me."

He stood back and took one of her hands in his. "I made something for you. Remember my surprise?"

She chuckled and followed him along the side of his property. "You mean writing me a song and professing your love wasn't enough?"

He lifted his chin playfully high. "Nope." He led her to an area of his yard where the trees opened up, inviting an incredible view, the Blue Ridge Mountains prominent and inspiring. "I built this for you."

Sophie was confused. "You built this view for me?"

He chuckled. "No, silly. Look behind you."

There on the edge of the hill sat a wooden bench, a brass plate offering the name Baby Bird Lookout.

Sophie ran her hand over the oak, smooth under her palm, not a flaw in sight. "It's beautiful."

Julian stood beside her and pointed down the hill. "You can see our spot from up here. I was going to leave it down there for you and tell you about it in my letter, but this is so much better."

She appreciated the view. And so much more than that. Some couples had songs. Sophie had a song *and* a special place in the mountains of Virginia where a scruffy looking man turned her heart from stone-cold to as warm as summer sunshine. She thought about the title of the song he'd written for her. It was true. She was the sun in his heart, and he was the sun in hers. "Oh, yeah? Well, you must've seen me walking a lot lately, then?"

He rubbed his jaw in a jeering sort of way. "Is that what you were doing? I thought you were trying to wear a trench through the path by the number of times you power walked by. I almost clocked you."

She feigned outrage as she jabbed him in the side. "Yeah, well, that was all your fault. I burned those calories in protest."

He leaned down to whisper into her ear. "You want to burn a few more? I've been fantasizing about making love to you on this bench since you got here." He rolled his eyes. "That's a lie. I've been fantasizing about it since I made it. I just never thought I'd get the opportunity." He pulled her close, his lips landing on hers, his tongue wasting no time to reacquaint and explore.

Sophie's inner thighs quivered, her nipples already hard, remembering the best sex she'd ever had. "Now? What about your father? What if he comes back?"

His hands finding her butt, Julian squeezed. "He said he wouldn't return unless I texted that I had spoken to you first."

"What if someone down below looks up and sees us."

He rested his forehead against hers. "Do you really care?" Without waiting for her to answer him, he lifted her tank top over her head, a cool breeze providing refreshment for her skin. And then came her bra, the tent beneath Julian's shorts getting larger. "Man, you've got great tits." He suckled one nipple while massaging the other with his thumb.

The next breath of wind that pushed through nearly knocked Sophie on her ass, her legs struggling to stand, a moisture factory working hard between her legs.

"Do you mind if I take these shorts off?"

Unable to speak, she nodded, giving him custody of her shorts and panties, which he threw to the side.

On full display, she worked the button and zipper on his shorts, letting them fall to the ground around his feet. He removed his own shirt.

"I really want to taste you right now. You okay with that?" He guided her down to the bench.

Leaves rustled in the trees like cheerleaders with pom-poms, offering their support as nature's audience. "Do what you gotta do, Bri." She opened her legs as he knelt in front of her, his mouth burying itself between her legs, his tongue finding her folds with amazing accuracy. As his tongue massaged her inner core, she arched her back and moaned, her hands lacing through his gorgeous locks. He lifted her hips up closer to his mouth, her legs draping over his shoulders. Up and down, in and out, he worked the most private regions of her body like a pro. An intense sensation started small but wound through her lower half like a mini twister until she cried out, "Oh my God," in rapture. Before Julian could bask in the glow of her, she pulled him up onto the bench and straddled him, her body refusing to let go of that orgasm or the man who'd given it to her.

With his hands on her hips, she lifted herself up and then down, his erection filling every square inch of her insides. He rubbed her nipples as she pumped more and more, until Julian's head dropped back, and his eyes rolled up in his head. "Jesus Christ, you're hot."

When he climaxed, she swore she did, too. Or maybe she never came down from the last one. She had never felt more sexual or aroused by anyone in her life.

All at once, Julian tipped his head up, his eyes wide. "Shit, Soph, I forgot to put a condom on."

With him still inside of her, she kissed his head and then his lips. "I just had my cycle a few days ago, and I'm on the pill." She kissed him again. "I think we're safe for now." A devilish thought tickled her mind. "But if you want to try this in the house, we can make use of those condoms." She offered him a catlike grin.

His breathing returning to normal, he smiled. "How about in my bed?" He tipped his head to the side. "In that hot tub over there, on the kitchen counter, and maybe even on the pool table in my game room. Once we call your security company, of course."

She sighed. "Of course. And that's a lot of places. Looks like I'm gonna have to stick around for a while."

He purred his answer. "If that's what will keep you around, I'll make love to you on every square inch of this property *and* yours." He buried his head in her breasts and then looked up at her, his eyes glimmering with tears. "I don't ever want to be without you again, Soph."

* * *

Eighteen months later ...

"You gettin' tired, or are you ready for some more music?" Julian asked his audience, his voice booming through the enormous speakers throughout the arena. The audience of 60,000 fans filled the smoky air with hoots and hollers in various forms, a few lucky ones stationed in the front rows, who stood awestruck. "Cause I'm just getting started."

Looking like a musical Adonis, Julian's smile stretched wide. His forehead was beaded with sweat and his cheeks fired up and ready to go, even after an hour of performing. "I want you all to know that you rock my world here in DC." More screams saturated the air as Julian sauntered across the stage in his tight jeans and equally snug T-shirt, thick plumes of smoke floating overhead, forming white clouds from the band's pyrotechnics. Flood lights swayed back and forth with their elongated arms, moving to the music, while an enormous screen in the background projected Julian as the giant he was.

He'd put on quite a show for his fans, and they were rewarding him verbally, even Lisa Pantera, who stood off to the side with her cameraman collecting sound bites after receiving her interview of a lifetime. The question "Where in the world is Julian Sommers?" had finally been answered. He was alive, and he was well. The story would bless the airways in a couple of weeks.

Two men ran out, each delivering a stool to center stage, a place where Julian would soon visit. "You know, a few years back, I thought my music career was over. Hell, I thought my life was over." The crowd quieted for the first time that evening as Julian paced the stage. "I'm sure you all know the story, as tragic as it was." He paused by his grand piano—and not a baby grand, either—one holding a bottle of water for him to wet his vocal cords, which he did a moment later. "But just when I thought there was no hope, someone came into my life. Someone *very* special." Wearing an endearing smile, he turned his focus backstage where Sophie stood, right next to Brian, Johnathan, Miranda (Johnathan's girlfriend, whom Sophie loved), and Charlie and Ginny, who had made a rare appearance for the occasion.

Sophie kissed her fingers and blew, sending her love to Julian across the way.

A moment later, one of those same roadies who had delivered a stool approached Sophie. "You ready?"

Anxiety bubbled in her stomach, already a little queasy these days.

He held his arm out for her to take, which she did, and together they walked the stage, their destination, one of those vacant stools. The minute Sophie came into view, the audience revved up with whistles and screams, the air electric.

Then Julian returned his gaze out over the 60,000 heads before him, his hand sweeping across the crowd. "I hope all of you have a special someone in your life." He strolled closer to Sophie. "That one person who picks you up when you need it most. That one person who shows you another way when you can't find one on your own. That one person who makes you ... *feel less like a mess.*" As if the audience knew that lyric all too well and the hit song attached to it climbing the charts, their cheering reached an almost unimaginable decibel.

Sophie wanted to cover her ears but knew that wouldn't be right. These people loved Julian just as much as they loved his hit song which made Sophie's heart smile every time she heard it.

With Sophie safely resting on one of the stools, Julian pivoted his body toward her. He lifted her hand to his mouth and kissed her knuckles, the same hand attached to the arm flashing his tattoo. Only now two tattoos decorated his ample bicep: the same eclipse that indicated a dark time in his life and, right above it, a heart with a sun inside it. *His future.* "Let me introduce you to the woman who changed my life. My beloved wife, Soph. The mother of our unborn daughter." He placed his hand over her small belly, the one that was growing each day.

With his acoustic guitar strapped around his neck and shoulders, he sat next to his wife, his eyes sending her all the love his heart could possibly give. He placed his microphone on a stand already lowered to just the right height. "Because, folks, she *is* the 'Sun in My Heart.'"

That did it. The crowd went wild, anticipation running on high-octane. Julian strummed his guitar, a few chords echoing into the mighty beyond. And then he sang to her, his voice perfect, his love and devotion lacing through every lyric.

Both of them lost and frayed by life, two souls had found each other. Broken and struggling, they sought strength and refuge in each other's hearts.

Never again would Sophie believe she was unlovable. And she'd make sure that Julian never again doubted himself, either. They were together now. They were a family, something Sophie had always longed for.

Her life was full.
Her future now bursting with possibilities.

# Tell me what you think ...

Authors are nothing without their readers. I would love to know what you think about *Sun in My Heart*.

Please consider leaving me a review (a few words are plenty) on Amazon, Goodreads, and/or BookBub. For self-published authors, reviews are so important.

Thank you for reading, and keep an eye out for my next project!

# About the Author

Since she was a little girl, award-winning author Tricia T. LaRochelle has been obsessed with tragic love stories. No beach reads for her. In a true love story, it's the struggles and the sacrifices that two people endure *and* overcome to be together that make a romance interesting and compelling.

Growing up in central Vermont, she has seen her share of tragedy but remains a hopeful romantic. She now lives in central Virginia, where she continues to foster the possibilities of how love can conquer all.

Sign up for her newsletter at TriciaLaRochelle.com for updates, announcements, and giveaways, or follow her on Facebook, Twitter, Instagram, Threads, or Pinterest.

 facebook.com/Tricia.larochelle

 instagram.com/larochelletricia

 threads.net/@Threads.net@larochelletricia

 pinterest.com/ttlarochelle

# Also by Tricia T. LaRochelle

**Sara Browne Series Romantic Suspense:**

**Flickering Heart - Book 1**

**Revive - Book 2**

**Handfast - Book 3**

**Bleeding Heart - A Holiday Romance - Book 4**

**Stand alone Contemporary Romances:**

**Sun in My Heart**

**Coming soon ... A Collision with Love**

# Acknowledgments

This book took me by storm. I went from not sure what I was going to write about, to fanatically typing away on my keyboard as though the words couldn't funnel through me fast enough. When that happens to an author, it's such a gift. The absolute best.

I really enjoyed getting to know Sophie and Julian. I loved them for their struggles and for their triumphs. I prefer flawed characters who grapple with themselves and their decisions, mainly because I believe that no one gets an easy ride in this life, but we all hope that through courage and love, we can find happiness as Sophie and Julian have.

When I first starting writing, I never thought I'd be where I am today. I can't say the journey was easy, but I can say it was worth every tear and moment of struggle to get where I am now. I've always said it takes a village to publish a book. And I have been lucky to have found qualified people in my corner.

Authors Michael Bowe, Craig Allen Heath, and Marta Moran Bishop, thank you for your unwavering support and helpful promotion. Your kindness sets you apart from the masses.

Melissa Shelton Harrison has been invaluable on my Sara Browne Series, as well as providing crucial input on *Sun in My Heart*. Her astute observations and insightful questions forced me to think about my characters on a deeper level, allowing me to provide my readers with a more profound experience. Her proofreading skills are another amazing talent of hers. I met Melissa nearly ten years ago when we were both just starting out, and I am so glad I did.

Thank you to my husband who is always a willing participant to read whatever I've conjured up. Bob still surprises me with his insight and keen sense of storytelling. My daughter-in-law, Hattie LaRochelle, is fast becoming my go-to for first-draft observations and proofreading skills that would put most people to shame.

My son, Ryan, is my clean-up guy, for he will find that hidden typo or phrase that doesn't quite work, even after all the rounds of editing are complete.

To Xuni.com, thank you for always providing the best looking website I could ask for. It doesn't matter what the newest change is, you respond quickly and thoroughly with your creative input.

To those amazing book bloggers, you people are the absolute best. I am so grateful to you for your promotion and your reviews. And to Amy at Indie Penn and Josette at Grey's Promotions for all your hard work getting my name and my work out there. You rock.

To my family and friends who may not work directly on my books but are always there to offer a positive "Way to go, *Mom*," or a friendly pat on the back, thank you from the bottom of my heart. You make this journey so much more fun and exciting.

She came in at the very end, but I would also like to thank Anne Tolpegin for her narration of *Sun in My Heart* for Audible. Venturing into something like Audible was a bit scary for me at first, but finding someone as talented as Anne set my mind at ease. She brought these characters to life on a level that still impresses and astounds me.

Finally, I want to thank you, my readers. I'd be nothing without you. I have always enjoyed connecting with people, and writing these stories has allowed me to do just that. Whenever I read a review by someone who was truly moved by my work, I am beyond touched. You people also rock my world!